许渊冲

枕上宋词

许渊冲 译

中国致公出版社

目录

辑一

浮生未歇

辑二 莫失莫忘

辑四

得闲忘机

辑五

半城烟沙

辑六

思归念远

辑一

浮生

未

歇

点绛唇 · 桃源 · 醉漾轻舟
秦观

醉漾轻舟，信流引到花深处。尘缘相误，无计花间住。
烟水茫茫，千里斜阳暮。山无数，乱红如雨。不记来时路。

Rouged Lips
Qin Guan

Drunk, at random I float
Along the stream my little boat.
By misfortune, among
The flowers I cannot stay long.

Misty waters outspread,
I find the slanting sun on turning my head,

And countless mountains high.

Red flowers fall in showers,

I don't remember the way I came by.

关键词

float：漂浮，轻盈走动，飘然移动。对译小舟轻"漾"。译者未用行船、开船之语，仅取漂浮之义，和 random（任意的）相辅相成，"信流"之美，引出"误入"之情，实在精妙。

among：在……当中，周围是。烟云缭绕、青山排列、落花飘动，而我则迷失其中。小小介词，独立成句，仿佛一个重音，节奏突变，让读者如临其境。

fall in showers：对译乱红"如雨"。showers，阵雨。用阵雨猛而急的特征，对译红花之"乱"，而不直接说"乱"。

译文

我乘着醉意，驾着小船在湖中荡漾。任凭流水将我引到花草深处。现实中的名利缠身，让我不能脱身，无法常住在这如花的仙境中。

烟云在水波中缭绕，斜阳的暮色染尽千里。两岸的青山排列无数。落花随风飘动，我仿佛迷失在雨境中，竟然不记得来时走过的路了。

秦 观

　　秦观，字少游，一字太虚，别号邗沟居士，高邮（今江苏高邮）人。既是"苏门四学士"中的一员，又是"苏门六君子"之一。长于议论，文丽思深，兼有诗、词、文赋、书法多方面的艺术才能，尤以婉约词驰名于世。词风上承柳永、晏几道，下开周邦彦、李清照。著有《淮海集》《淮海词》《劝善录》《逆旅集》等。

满庭芳 · 山抹微云
秦观

山抹微云，天连衰草，画角声断谯门。暂停征棹，聊共引离尊。多少蓬莱旧事，空回首、烟霭纷纷。斜阳外，寒鸦万点，流水绕孤村。

销魂。当此际，香囊暗解，罗带轻分。谩赢得，青楼薄幸名存。此去何时见也？襟袖上、空惹啼痕。伤情处，高城望断，灯火已黄昏。

Courtyard Full of Fragrance
Qin Guan

A belt of clouds girds mountains high
And withered grass spreads to the sky.
The painted horn at the watchtower blows.

Before my boat sails up, Let's drink a farewell cup.

How many things do I recall in bygone days,

All lost in mist and haze! Beyond the setting sun I see but dots

of crows

And that around a lonely village water flows.

I'd call to mind the soul-consuming hour

When I took off your perfume purse unseen

And loosened your silk girdle in your bower.

All this has merely won me in the Mansion Green

The name of fickle lover. Now I'm a rover, O when can I see

you again?

My tears are shed in vain; In vain they wet my sleeves.

It grieves, My heart to find your bower out of sight;

It's lost at dusk in city light.

关键词

watchtower blows：瞭望台的疾风，对译"声断谯门"。声
为何断？因疾风而断。译者补齐了画面，再现原词的意境美，且
blows 又和下文的 flows 押韵，做到了音美。

soul-consuming hour：对译"销魂"一词，此处直译为"灵魂
消耗的时刻"，比单单的 consuming hour（令人着迷的时刻）更
契合语境。

in vain：徒劳的、枉然的，对译"空惹"。连着两个"in
vain"，语气加重——我的泪空流，眼泪又白白地打湿了我的衣襟，

双重的伤情。

译文

　　山峰将微云抹开，氤氲缭绕，极目天涯，衰草连绵，延伸到天边。城门楼上的号角声，时断时续。在我起航前，请共饮这杯离别酒。再回首，多少旧事化作云烟。夕阳下，寒鸦点缀了天空，流水围绕着村落。

　　人断魂。悲伤之际，轻轻解开你的衣带，悄悄藏起你的香囊。就让我背负薄幸之名。这一别，不知何时再见？离别的泪水浸湿了衣襟与袖口。最是伤心时，城郭消失在天边，万家灯火照亮了这个黄昏。

浣溪沙 · 簌簌衣巾落枣花

苏轼

簌簌衣巾落枣花，村南村北响缫车。牛衣古柳卖黄瓜。

酒困路长惟欲睡，日高人渴漫思茶。敲门试问野人家。

Silk-washing Stream

Su Shi

Date flowers fall in showers on my hooded head;

At both ends of the village wheels are spinning thread;

A straw-cloaked man sells cucumbers beneath a willow tree.

Wine-drowsy when the road is long, I yearn for bed;

Throat parched when the sun is high, I long for tea.

I knock at a farmer's door to see what he'll treat me.

关键词

hooded：戴兜帽、头巾的。on my hooded head 译为落在我的头巾上，此处为意译，对译"衣巾"，head 一词与下文的 thread、bed 等押韵。

long for：渴望、极想。对译"漫思"茶。漫，随意，极言口渴，想随意去哪儿找点茶喝，译者特选用了 long for 这一程度更深的词语，情感表达得恰如其分。

译文

往来的行人身上落满了枣花，整个村子都响起了缫丝的声音，一位身穿蓑衣的农民，在古老的柳树下叫卖着黄瓜。

酒后困顿，遥远的路途让人昏然欲睡，当午的太阳让人口渴难耐。索性敲开野外的村户，询问可否讨杯茶喝。

苏　轼

苏轼，字子瞻、和仲，号东坡居士，眉州眉山（今四川省眉山市）人，与父苏洵、弟苏辙并称"三苏"。他是北宋中期名震朝野的文坛领袖，在诗、词、散文、书法、绘画等艺术领域，都取得旷古烁今的杰出成就，是名冠两宋的全能型才子，著有《东坡乐府》等。

行香子·冬思·携手江村
苏轼

携手江村，梅雪飘裙。情何限、处处消魂。故人不见，旧曲重闻。向望湖楼，孤山寺，涌金门。

寻常行处，题诗千首，绣罗衫、与拂红尘。别来相忆，知是何人。有湖中月，江边柳，陇头云。

Song of Incense
Su Shi

We visited the riverside village hand in hand,
Letting snow-like mume flowers on silk dress fall.
How can I stand the soul-consuming fairy land!
Now separated from you for years long,
Hearing the same old song, Can I forget the lakeside hall,

The temple on the Lonely Hill and Golden Gate waves overfill?

Wherever we went on whatever day,

We have written a thousand lines.

The silken sleeves would sweep the dust away.

Since we parted, who would often think of you?

The moon which on the lake shines,

The lakeside willow trees, The cloud and breeze.

关键词

sweep the dust away：对译"拂红尘"，the dust 取"灰尘"意，全句意为"用罗衫拂去这些诗上的尘土才能看清"。译者在此取"红尘"的本义，为浅化之法，也有双关之意。

breeze：微风、和风。The cloud and breeze 对译"陇头云"。"湖中月，江边柳，陇头云"不是泛指，而是说的西湖、钱塘江和城西南诸名山的景物，本是词人与友人在杭州时常游赏的，它们对他的相忆，意为召唤他回去了。故而译者并未直译"陇头"为"小山丘、田埂"。

译文

与友人共游江畔村庄，梅花的花瓣像雪一样飘落到裙衫上。止不住的情感，让人无限愁苦。老友们不在，听到旧曲，让人不禁回想起一同走过的望湖楼、孤山寺、涌金门。

所到之处，写下千首诗作。用衣袖拂去墙上题诗的尘土。离别之后，还有谁在思念我呢？是我们一起看过的湖中月、江边柳、孤山云。

行香子·述怀·清夜无尘
苏轼

清夜无尘，月色如银。酒斟时、须满十分。浮名浮利，虚苦劳神。叹隙中驹，石中火，梦中身。

虽抱文章，开口谁亲。且陶陶、乐尽天真。几时归去，作个闲人。对一张琴，一壶酒，一溪云。

Song of Pilgrimage
Su Shi

Stainless is the clear night; The moon is silver bright.

Fill my wine cup, Till it brims up!

Why toil with pain, For wealth and fame in vain?

Time flies as a steed white

Passes a gap in flight. Like a spark in the dark. Or a dream of moonbeam.

Though I can write, Who thinks I'm right?

Why not enjoy, Like a mere boy?

So I would be, A man carefree.

I would be mute before my lute; It would be fine in face of wine; I would be proud to cleave the cloud.

关键词

toil with pain：辛勤苦干，对译"虚苦劳神"，与下句的 in vain（徒劳的）相对，且押韵。译者还变换句式，以问句译陈述句，加强了肯定语气。

like a mere boy：mere，纯粹的，全句对译"乐尽天真"，直译为"像个纯真的孩子"。本句也变换了句式，以反问句译陈述句，加强肯定语气。

a man carefree：对译"闲人"，译文特选用 carefree(无忧无虑的，无牵挂的) 一词，并加词 I would be（我想做），表达了词人对归隐田园生活的向往。

译文

夜里，空气清新，月色皎洁。美酒须满杯，开怀须畅饮。名利如浮云，徒教人劳苦费神。人生不过像快马飞驰过隙缝，像击石迸出的火花，更像是一场梦。

我虽满腹才华，说出来，谁才是知音呢？姑且无忧无虑、快乐单纯地过日子吧。何时归隐田园，做个闲人。自弹一张琴，自饮一壶酒，自赏一片云。

蝶恋花·春景·花褪残红青杏小
苏轼

花褪残红青杏小。燕子飞时，绿水人家绕。枝上柳绵吹又少。天涯何处无芳草。

墙里秋千墙外道。墙外行人，墙里佳人笑。笑渐不闻声渐悄。多情却被无情恼。

Butterflies in Love with Flowers
Su Shi

Red flowers fade, green apricots appear still small,
When swallows pass
Over blue water that surrounds the garden wall.
Most willow catkins have been blown away, alas!
But there is no place where grows no sweet grass.

Without the wall there is a path, within a swing.

A passer-by

Hears a fair maiden's laughter in the garden ring.

The ringing laughter fades to silence by and by;

For the enchantress the enchanted can only sigh.

关键词

no place where: 此句对译"天涯何处无芳草",译者用了"no place……no"的双重否定句式以表肯定,对应原词的"何处……无"句式,十分工整,且加了 but 一词以表转折,形美而意赅。

by and by: 不久以后,逐渐。译者将"笑"与"声"、"渐不闻"和"渐悄"均合起来翻译,故而将状语 by and by 后置,还和 passer-by 押韵,译文十分精巧。

the enchantress: 迷人的女人,即墙里佳人。the enchanted,被迷住的人,即墙外行人。此处为意译,对译"多情"与"无情",以人物指代情绪,更简洁准确。

译文

花儿褪尽残红,树梢上长出小小的青杏。燕子低飞,绿水绕着村落流动。柳枝上的柳絮被春风吹落,越来越少,但是这世上到处都有茂盛的芳草。

围墙里面,一位少女正在荡秋千。连墙外的行人,都能听到墙里传出的笑声。笑声渐渐变小,墙外行人的心情也随之低落,仿佛自己的多情被无情的少女辜负了。

丑奴儿·书博山道中壁·少年不识愁滋味

辛弃疾

少年不识愁滋味，爱上层楼。爱上层楼，为赋新词强说愁。

而今识尽愁滋味，欲说还休。欲说还休，却道天凉好个秋！

Song of Ugly Slave

Xin Qiji

While young, I knew no grief I could not bear;

I'd like to go upstair.

I'd like to go upstair

To write new verses with a false despair.

I know what grief is now that I am old;

I would not have it told.

I would not have it told,

But only say I'm glad that autumn's cold.

关键词

grief：悲伤、伤心事。no grief I could not bear，对译"不识愁滋味"，此处为意译，直译为"没有无法忍受的悲伤"。

with a false despair：带着一种虚假的绝望，对译"强说愁"。

have it told：直译为"将它说出来"。I would not have it told，对译"欲说还休"，想说却无法说出口，遵循了原文的叠句、重复，强调了词人的烦闷、无奈。

译文

年少时不理解忧愁的滋味，只爱登高望远。站在高楼上，为了写出一首新词强行装作愁闷。

而今我已历尽沧桑，早就尝尽人间辛酸，想说却说不出来了。愁怨无法诉说，却只道，好一个凉爽的秋天啊！

辛弃疾

　　辛弃疾，原字坦夫，后改字幼安，号稼轩，历城（今济南市历城区）人。杰出的豪放派词人、将领，有"词中之龙"之誉，与苏轼合称"苏辛"，与李清照并称"济南二安"。其词多念国事，慷慨悲歌，亦有清新隽永、婉丽妩媚之作。著有《稼轩长短句》。

卜算子·咏梅·驿外断桥边
陆游

驿外断桥边，寂寞开无主。已是黄昏独自愁，更著风和雨。
无意苦争春，一任群芳妒。零落成泥碾作尘，只有香如故。

Song of Divination
Ode to the Mume Blossom
Lu You

Beside the broken bridge and outside the post hall
A flower is blooming forlorn.
Saddened by her solitude at nightfall,
By wind and rain she's further torn.

Let other flowers their envy pour!

To spring she lays no claim.

Fallen in mud and ground to dust, she seems no more,

But her fragrance is still the same.

关键词

forlorn: 被遗弃的，孤独的。"花儿孤独地绽放"对译"寂寞开无主"，"无主"既有无人照看，也有无人欣赏之义，forlorn 一词的丰富含义，准确点出了词人以花自况的凄苦心境。

further torn: 进一步被撕裂、折断。译者加词翻译"更著风和雨"——"又遭到风吹雨打而飘落四方"，补足了内外交困的情境。

lays no claim: 没有索要什么，对译"无意"。看似是对春天"无意"，实际是无意与百花争夺春色。

译文

驿站外的断桥边，梅花孤单地绽放，无人照顾和欣赏。暮色中无依无靠的梅花，还要经受风雨的摧残。

本就无意费力与百花争奇斗艳，还惹来群芳嫉妒。即便花瓣凋零被碾作尘土，傲人的清香依旧存在。

陆 游

　　陆游，字务观，号放翁，越州山阴（今浙江绍兴）人。诗、词、散文俱佳，兼擅书法。一生作诗无数，仅保存下来的就有九千三百余首，诗风豪放，气势雄浑，颇类李白，故有"小太白"之誉，与杨万里、范成大、尤袤合称"中兴四大诗人"。著有《放翁词》等。

声声慢·寻寻觅觅
李清照

　　寻寻觅觅，冷冷清清，凄凄惨惨戚戚。乍暖还寒时候，最难将息。三杯两盏淡酒，怎敌他、晚来风急？雁过也，正伤心，却是旧时相识。

　　满地黄花堆积。憔悴损，如今有谁堪摘？守着窗儿，独自怎生得黑？梧桐更兼细雨，到黄昏、点点滴滴。这次第，怎一个愁字了得！

Slow, Slow Tune
Li Qingzhao

I look for what I miss; I know not what it is.

I feel so sad, so drear, so lonely, without cheer.

How hard is it, To keep me fit, In this lingering cold!

Hardly warmed up, By cup on cup, Of wine so dry,

O how could I, Endure at dusk the drift, Of wind so swift?

It breaks my heart, alas! To see the wild geese pass,

For they are my acquaintances of old.

The ground is covered with yellow flowers,

Faded and fallen in showers. Who will pick them up now?

Sitting alone at the window, how

Could I but quicken

The pace of darkness that won't thicken?

On plane's broad leaves a fine rain drizzles

As twilight grizzles.O what can I do with a grief, Beyond belief!

关键词

so sad, so drear, so lonely：“凄凄惨惨戚戚”三对双声叠韵词，用“so+adj”三对排比词组对译，“如此悲伤，如此阴郁，如此孤独”，词人凄苦、悲凉的心境展露无遗，原词的音韵之美也表现得淋漓尽致。前两句中，“miss”与“觅”音似，“cheer”与“戚”音似，以音美传达了意美。

lingering cold：对译“乍暖还寒”一词。此词作于秋天，本应为“乍寒还暖”，故词人用“乍暖还寒”非写一季之候，而是写一日之晨。秋日清晨，朝阳初出，但晓寒犹重，秋风砭骨。lingering意为“逗留的”，lingering cold——“逗留的寒冷”，灵动有趣。

acquaintances of old：对译“旧时相识”，在异乡再见大雁，都是“老熟人”了，睹物相思。

译文

想要把失去的都找回来，却什么也没有，让人忧愁苦闷。秋天忽暖忽冷，最难休养调理。三两杯小酒，怎能抵挡那夜晚的寒风。大雁飞过头顶，让人更伤心，因为它们都是当年为我传递书信的旧日相识。

菊花残落满地，花朵样子憔悴，让谁忍心采摘？孤独地守在窗前，一个人怎么熬到天黑？细雨打在梧桐叶上，到了黄昏时分，还是滴滴答答的。这光景，怎是一个"愁"字能说得清的？

李清照

　　李清照，号易安居士，宋齐州章丘人，虽为闺阁中人，却以锦绣词章屹立于两宋词林，历千年而不衰，被后人称为"千古第一才女"。著有《漱玉词》。

浣溪沙 · 二月和风到碧城
晏几道

二月和风到碧城，万条千缕绿相迎。舞烟眠雨过清明。

妆镜巧眉偷叶样，歌楼妍曲借枝名。晚秋霜霰莫无情。

Silk-washing Stream
Yan Jidao

The gentle breeze of second moon has greened the town.

Thousands of your branches swing and sway up and down.

You dance in mist and sleep in rain on Mourning Day.

Ladies pencil their brows to imitate your leaf.

Songstresses sing your song to diminish their grief.

Late autumn frost, why delight in willows'decay?

关键词

　　town：城镇、市镇。"碧城"是丛丛柳树的形象化比喻，故译者以动词译名词，has greened the town，"（和风）已经染绿了城镇"。

　　Mourning Day：哀悼日，对译"清明"。译者未用 the pure brightness day（清明节），而将其浅化翻译，更利于有文化差异的西方读者理解。

　　imitate：模仿。imitate your leaf 对译"偷叶样"，此处的"偷"即"模仿"之意，词人巧妙地以眉和柳叶将人和物联系起来，译者则将其浅化译出，点明了原词的本义。

译文

　　二月春风将满城吹绿，千万条绿柳迎风飘动，在晴烟轻霭中舞动，在霏霏细雨中安眠，就在这柔和的景象中，不知不觉已过了清明。

　　美人对镜梳妆，照着柳叶描眉，歌楼酒曲也用柳枝作为曲名。待到晚秋，凌霜请莫摧残这寥落的绿色。

晏几道

晏几道，字叔原，号小山，晏殊第七子。性孤傲，与其父合称"二晏"，词风似父而造诣过之。工于言情，其小令语言清丽，感情深挚，是婉约派的重要词人，有《小山词》存世。

柳梢青·送卢梅坡·泛菊杯深
刘过

泛菊杯深,吹梅角远,同在京城。聚散匆匆,云边孤雁,水上浮萍。

教人怎不伤情? 觉几度、魂飞梦惊。后夜相思,尘随马去,月逐舟行。

Green Willow Tips

Farewell to a Friend

Liu Guo

Drinking a cupful of chrysanthemum wine

And hearing flute songs of mume flowers fine,

We were then under capital's roofs.

We' ve met and now in haste we part,

Like lonely swan passing the clouds with speed

Or on the water floating duckweed.

How can grief not come like a stream?

How many times have we been awakened from dream

With broken heart?

I will miss you in the deep night

Like dust raised by horsehoofs

Or the boat followed by the moon bright.

关键词

cupful：满杯，对译"杯深"。深，言酌酒之满，把畅怀酣饮的情形描写了出来，故译者未以"深"译，而以"满杯"译之。

stream：一连串，源源不断（的事情）。like a stream 为译者加词，修饰 grief（伤情）的绵绵不绝，契合原词的情境。

horsehoofs：马蹄，此处译者用了"提喻"的修辞手法，以马蹄对译马。该句直译为"就像马蹄踏起的尘土"，场景更为具象可感。

译文

我们曾经都在京城，共饮菊花酒，一起郊游赏梅。没想到聚散匆匆，我们就像天边的孤雁，水上的浮萍，各自飘摇。

这叫人怎么不感伤？曾有几次在梦里相会，惊喜而醒。后半夜却因思念无法入眠，恨不能像飞尘跟随在马后，像明月伴你行舟。

乌鹊将栖萋萋溪烟松上时依声何蒙起风在家高枝

梅曹雪西风林晚

鸿翥平

刘 过

刘过，字改之，号龙洲道人，吉州太和（今江西泰和县）人，四次应试不中，布衣终身。词风与辛弃疾相近，与刘克庄、刘辰翁享有"辛派三刘"之誉，又与刘仙伦合称为"庐陵二布衣"。著有《龙洲集》《龙洲词》《龙洲道人诗集》，现存词七十余首。

蝶恋花·送春·楼外垂杨千万缕
朱淑真

楼外垂杨千万缕，欲系青春，少住春还去。犹自风前飘柳絮，随春且看归何处？

绿满山川闻杜宇，便做无情，莫也愁人苦。把酒送春春不语，黄昏却下潇潇雨。

Butterflies in Love with Flowers

Farewell to Spring

Zhu Shuzhen

Thousands of willow twigs beyond my bower sway;

They try to retain spring, but she won't stay

For long and goes away.

In vernal breeze the willow down still wafts with grace;

It tries to follow spring to find her dwelling place.

Hills and rills greened all over, I hear cuckoos sing;
Feeling no grief, why should they give me a sharp sting?
With wine cup in hand, I ask spring who won't reply.
When evening grizzles,
A cold rain drizzles.

关键词

retain：保留。此句对译"欲系青春"，青春指大好春光，隐指词人的青春年华。译者以 retain 译"系"，写出了垂柳力图挽留春天的缱绻多情。

wafts with grace：优雅地飘荡。wafts，飘荡。译者加了 with grace 修饰了柳絮依然飘飞的姿态，也是为了凑韵，和 place 押尾韵。

sharp sting：剧烈的痛苦，对译"愁人苦"。译者用了极苦之词烘托出即使是无情之人，目接耳闻这芳春消逝之景，怕也要愁苦不已了。

译文

楼外垂挂着千万条柳枝，我想留住这大好春光，可春景只停留片刻便不见踪影。只有柳絮随风飘舞，它想随着春风看看春归何处。

满山的绿色，有杜鹃啼鸣。就算鸟无情感，那凄厉的叫声岂不也叫人愁苦。举杯送别春天，春天沉默不语，黄昏时分忽然下起了潇潇细雨。

朱淑真

朱淑真，号幽栖居士，浙中海宁（一说钱塘）人，南宋著名女词人，与李清照齐名。生于仕宦之家，幼颖慧，博通经史，能文善画，精晓音律，尤工诗词。后因与丈夫志趣不合，抑郁早逝，其余生平皆不可考。传其过世后，父母将其生前文稿付之一炬，现存《断肠诗集》《断肠词》则为劫后余篇。

浣溪沙·一曲新词酒一杯
晏殊

一曲新词酒一杯，去年天气旧亭台。夕阳西下几时回？

无可奈何花落去，似曾相识燕归来。小园香径独徘徊。

Silk-washing Stream
Yan Shu

A song filled with new words, a cup filled with old wine,

The bower is last year's , the weather is as fine.

Will last year reappear as the sun on decline?

Deeply I sigh for the fallen flowers in vain;

Vaguely I seem to know the swallows come again.

In fragrant garden path alone I still remain.

关键词

old wine：旧酒，对译"酒一杯"。此处译者加了 old 一词，与前文的"new words（新词）"对仗工整。

as fine：一样，此处为意译，对译"去年天气"。译者清晰明了地交代了旧时情境如眼前这般热闹，生动传神。

remain：逗留，留下。译者以被动的"留下"对译主动的"徘徊"，伤春的哀愁之情更显。

译文

一曲新词伴一杯美酒，还是跟去年一样的天气，还是在这熟悉的楼阁。西下的夕阳何时才能回来？

花落无情让人无可奈何，燕子归来让人似曾相识。我独自在这花香小径里留恋徘徊。

晏 殊

晏殊，字同叔，抚州临川（今江西抚州）人。以词著于文坛，尤擅小令，风格清雅婉丽、雍容温润，与其子晏几道被称为"大晏""小晏"，又与欧阳修并称"晏欧"；亦工诗善文，原有集，已散佚。存世有《珠玉词》《晏元献遗文》《类要》残本。

浣溪沙 · 一向年光有限身
晏殊

一向年光有限身，等闲离别易销魂。酒筵歌席莫辞频。

满目山河空念远，落花风雨更伤春。不如怜取眼前人。

Silk-washing Stream

Yan Shu

What can a short-lived man do with the fleeting year
And soul-consuming separations from his dear?
Refuse no banquet when fair singing girls appear!

With hills and rills in sight, I miss the far-off in vain.
How can I bear the fallen blooms in wind and rain!
Why not enjoy the fleeting pleasure now again?

关键词

　　fleeting：飞逝的，短暂的。"一向年光"意为片刻的时光，译者以 the fleeting year 译之，十分准确，且 year 与下文的 dear、appear 押韵。

　　pleasure：快乐、乐事。此句对译"不如怜取眼前人"，译者以反问句译陈述句，以快乐的情绪代指眼前人，加强了要珍惜眼前人的肯定语气。

译文

　　人生短暂，无端的别离特别容易让人惆怅。不要因为害怕这种感伤而推辞酒宴，应当对酒当歌，开怀畅饮。

　　满眼的辽阔河山，却无处寄托思绪。看到风雨中凋落的残花，更感慨春天易逝。不如好好怜惜眼前人。

花犯 · 赋水仙 · 楚江湄
周密

楚江湄，湘娥乍见，无言洒清泪，淡然春意。空独倚东风，芳思谁寄。凌波路、冷秋无际，香云随步起。漫记得、汉宫仙掌，亭亭明月底。

冰弦写怨更多情，骚人恨，枉赋芳兰幽芷。春思远，谁叹赏、国香风味。相将共、岁寒伴侣，小窗净，沉烟熏翠袂。幽梦觉，涓涓清露，一枝灯影里。

Invaded by Flowers

To the Daffodil

Zhou Mi

By the southern rivershore

Like the princess you appear; Silent, you shed tear on tear.

You care for spring no more.In vain on eastern breeze you lean.

To whom will you send fragrance green?

You seem to tread on waves to hear cold autumn's sighs;

After your steps fragrant clouds rise.

To what avail should you, Recall the fairy with a plate of dew,

Who stands fair and bright in the moonlight?

The icy strings reveal the grief of lovesick heart.

The poet regrets to have sung of orchids and grass,

But keep you apart. Your vernal thoughts go far away.

Who would enjoy the fragrance of bygone days?

Why not share with me the quiet window you've seen,

Where incense perfumes your sleeves green?

Awake from my sweet dream, alas!

I find by candlelight a part of you, Steeped in clear dew.

关键词

fragrance green：芳香的绿色，对译"芳思"，美好的情思。译者加了 green 一词，一则与上文的 lean 押韵，二则也与上文的"春意"呼应。

a plate of dew：一盘露水。汉宫仙掌是指汉武帝刘彻曾在建章宫前造神明台，上铸铜柱、铜仙人，手托承露盘以储甘露。译者因此典故，浅化译之。

quiet window：对译"小窗净"，译者以 quiet（素净的）译之，传达了"小轩窗"的东方之美。

译文

　　湘江河岸，忽然看见湘妃，清泪涟涟。她散发着淡然的春意，她在东风中独自伫立，美好的情思跟谁说？她步态轻盈，带着无边的秋意，香气随着她的步履飘动。徒记得，当年汉宫里承接甘露的金铜仙人，独自立在月光下。

　　琵琶将愁怨弹奏得更多情，屈原在《离骚》中赞美芳香幽雅的兰芷，却不提及水仙的高洁。谁叹赏她的国色天香？谁能理解她在冬日里的陪伴？明净的小窗里，我为她点燃沉香。隐约的梦境中，只见她一身清流，娉婷立在灯影中。

周　密

　　周密，字公谨，号草窗，吴兴（今浙江湖州）人，南宋覆灭后，入元不仕。能诗词，擅书画，词作典雅浓丽、格律严谨，与吴文英（号梦窗）齐名，时人号为"二窗"。著述繁富，留存诗词集有《草窗旧事》《萍洲渔笛谱》《云烟过眼录》《浩然斋雅谈》等，并编有《绝妙好词笺》。笔记体史学著作《武林旧事》《齐东野语》《癸辛杂识》等，是反映宋代杭州风情及社会生活的重要史料。

水龙吟·采药径·云屏漫锁空山
葛长庚

云屏漫锁空山，寒猿啼断松枝翠。芝英安在，术苗已老，徒劳屐齿。应记洞中，凤箫锦瑟，镇常歌吹。怅苍苔路杳，石门信断，无人问、溪头事。

回首暝烟无际，但纷纷、落花如泪。多情易老，青鸾何处，书成难寄。欲问双娥，翠蝉金凤，向谁娇媚。想分香旧恨，刘郎去后，一溪流水。

Water Dragon Chant
Pick Herbs
Ge Changgeng

Clouds veil the empty mountains like a screen;
Cold monkeys cry on pine branches green.

Where is the wonderful grass, And oldened seed? Alas!

I've tried to find them, but in vain.

Does the fairy cave still remain?

Do fairies often blow their phoenix flute,

And play on broidered lute?

I sigh for the way is covered with moss,

No message comes from the stone gate, I'm at a loss.

The fairies would be hard to seek;

Would they lead me along the creek?

I turn my head, a boundless plain appears,

And petals shed like tears.

Lovers are easy to grow old.

Have they heard, Where is the blue bird

To bring to them a word? I would ask the fair maid

For whom the golden phoenix and green jade

Displaying their charm, are displayed.

When the lover wakes from his dream,

What's left is only fallen petals on the stream.

关键词

fairy cave：仙人洞。此句对译"应记洞中"，译者以问句译陈述句，并结合词人学道的经历，加了 fairy（神仙）一词，表意更准确。

the blue bird：特指蓝色知更鸟，即青鸟，对译"青鸾"。青鸾本是仙家信使，"不见青鸾"，也就是不得成仙的消息。

fallen petals：落花。此句暗含曹操临死前分香与诸位夫人这一典故，译者以溪中落花代指，虚实结合，译出了幽明殊途之憾。

译文

浮云环绕空山宛若屏风，山间猿啼哀婉，松枝愈发苍翠。昔日珍惜的灵芝草药已无迹可寻，术苗也枯朽不能入药，采药人踏遍群山却是徒劳。还记得洞中仙境鼓瑟吹笙，歌舞升平的光景，如今却苍苔遍布，无人还记得当年溪畔遇仙引入桃源的往事。

仙境如今难寻，回头只见渺渺暮烟纷纷落花。岁月催人老，信使青鸾从未送来仙境的讯息。想要问问两位仙子，那发间插着的金凤钗，那份娇媚，如今又是为了谁。遥想曹操去世前分香给诸位夫人的遗恨，再看看刘晨、阮肇二人离开仙境后，空有溪水潺潺，寂寞地奔流。

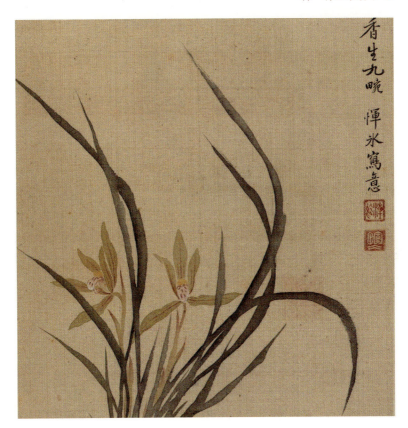

葛长庚

葛长庚，字白叟，号海琼子，世称紫清先生，海南琼山人。十六岁离家云游，养真于儋州松林岭，二十三岁只身渡海到各地求师，最后入住武夷山止止庵，师从道教南宗四世祖陈楠，尽得其道术。工于诗词，文词清亮高绝，著有《海琼集》《罗浮山志》等。

玉楼春·春景·东城渐觉风光好
宋祁

东城渐觉风光好，縠皱波纹迎客棹。绿杨烟外晓寒轻，红杏枝头春意闹。

浮生长恨欢娱少，肯爱千金轻一笑。为君持酒劝斜阳，且向花间留晚照。

Spring in Jade Pavilion
Song Qi

The scenery is getting fine east of the town;

The rippling water greets boats rowing up and down.

Beyond green willows morning chill is growing mild;

On pink apricot branches spring is running wild.

In our floating life scarce are pleasures we seek after.

How can we value gold above a hearty laughter?

I raise wine cup to ask the slanting sun to stay

And leave among the flowers its departing ray.

关键词

getting fine：一个 getting，对译最为得神的"渐"字，将那分明又有层次的芳春美景一一引了出来。

rippling：使起涟漪，使呈波状起伏。縠皱波纹，形容波纹细如皱纱，以 rippling water 译之，波纹骤起之景具体可感。

rowing up and down：上上下下地划动。译者加了 up and down 一词，补充描绘了因波而动的行船之貌。

mild：轻微的，温暖的。growing mild，渐渐温暖。此句直译为"绿柳外，晨寒渐暖"。

running wild：野蛮生长，对译红艳艳的杏花簇绽枝头的景象。"春意闹"，春天的气象已浓盛。

译文

漫步城东，感受到越来越近的好春光，仿佛皱纱的湖面上尽是游船泛舟。新绿的杨柳一排排宛若云烟，清晨的寒意渐渐褪去，杏花开满枝头，充满了生机。

总是抱怨人生欢愉太少，谁又肯用千金换取会心的一笑？让我为你举杯奉劝夕阳，请它在花丛间多停留些时间吧。

半夜歌风开露井一枝干
莩损春心
瓯香馆临宋人纨扇本
白云外史寿平

宋　祁

　　宋祁，字子京，小字选郎，安州安陆（今属湖北）人，后迁开封雍丘（今河南杞县）。北宋天圣二年，与胞兄宋庠同举进士，礼部本拟定宋祁第一、宋庠第三，但章献皇后觉得弟弟不能超越兄长，遂定宋庠为状元，而把宋祁放在第十位，时称"二宋"。曾与欧阳修等合修《新唐书》，诗词语言工丽，因《玉楼春》词中有"红杏枝头春意闹"句，世称"红杏尚书"。

西江月·世事短如春梦
朱敦儒

世事短如春梦，人情薄似秋云。不须计较苦劳心，万事原来有命。

幸遇三杯酒好，况逢一朵花新。片时欢笑且相亲，明日阴晴未定。

The Moon over the West River
Zhu Dunru

Life is as short as a spring dream;
Love is fleeting like autumn stream.
Don't on gain or loss speculate!
We can't avoid our fate.
I'm lucky to have three cups of good wine.

What's more,I can enjoy fresh flower.

Make merry in laughter for an hour.

Who knows if tomorrow it will be fine.

关键词

fleeting: 短暂的、飞逝的，对译人情之"薄"。Love is fleeting，译文将词人值此暮年之时，回首少年的欢情，顿觉遥远和飞逝的辛酸全盘托出。

speculate: 猜测，推测。

avoid our fate: 此句直译为"我们无法逃避命运"。"原来"二字，透露出一种无可奈何的情绪，又隐含几分激愤。译者以一个can't avoid（无法逃避）将这心境表达得十分准确。

make merry in laughter: 以笑为乐。make merry，作乐。词人得乐且乐的自我安慰得以表达。

译文

世事短暂恍如春日的一场好梦，人情凉薄好似秋空轻淡的浮云。不必计较自己的辛苦操劳，所有的事本来就已命中注定。

有幸遇到三杯好酒，又看见一朵刚开的鲜花。片刻的欢欣总是能够让人感到亲切，至于明天会发生什么就不得而知了。

朱敦儒

朱敦儒，字希真，洛阳人，有"词俊"之名，与"诗俊"陈与义等并称"洛中八俊"。在两宋词史上，能比较完整地表现出自我一生行藏出处、心态情感变化的，除朱敦儒之外，就只有后来的辛弃疾了。著有《岩壑老人诗文》，已佚；今存词集《樵歌》，也称《太平樵歌》，其词语言流畅，清新自然。

踏莎行·芳心苦·杨柳回塘
贺铸

杨柳回塘，鸳鸯别浦，绿萍涨断莲舟路。断无蜂蝶慕幽香，红衣脱尽芳心苦。

返照迎潮，行云带雨，依依似与骚人语。当年不肯嫁春风，无端却被秋风误。

Treading on Grass

To Lotus

He Zhu

On winding pool with willows dim, At narrow strait the lovebirds swim.

Green duckweeds float, Barring the way of lotus-picking boat.

Nor butterflies nor bees love fragrance from the withered trees.

When her red petals fall apart, The lotus bloom's bitter at heart.

The setting sun greets rising tide, The floating clouds bring rain.

The swaying lotus seems to confide, Her sorrow to the poet in vain.

Then she would not be wed to vernal breeze.

What could she do now autumn drives away wild geese?

关键词

narrow strait：狭窄的水道，对译"别浦（江河的支流入水口）"。译者将其具体化，浅化译之，更易于理解。

lovebirds：爱情鸟，对译"鸳鸯"，译文明白晓畅。

the setting sun：落日，对译"返照（夕阳的回光）"。落日的余晖返照在荡漾的水波之上，迎接着潮水。落日一词，言简意赅，却不失情境。

confide：吐露、倾诉。译文补足了主语——"the swaying lotus（那摇曳的莲花）"，她似乎在向诗人倾诉她的悲伤，而这只不过是徒劳罢了。这里显然是词人以莲花自比，香草、美人、贤士三位一体的典故，译文把握得十分到位。

译文

杨柳环绕着池塘，一对鸳鸯在江中戏水。满池的浮萍阻断了采莲人的路。荷花的幽香引不来蜂蝶，花瓣落了，露出苦涩的莲心。

夕阳的回光照着晚潮，流动的云层带来的密密细雨，无情地打在荷花上。那随风摆动的荷花，好像对我倾诉着万般衷肠：当时不肯在春天开放，如今只能在秋风里受尽凄凉。

贺 铸

贺铸，字方回，自号庆湖遗老，卫州共城（今河南辉县）人。出身贵族世家，宋太祖贺皇后族孙，所娶亦宗室之女。能诗文，尤擅词，其词风格丰富多样，兼有豪放、婉约二派之长。著有《庆湖遗老集》《东山词》。

临江仙 · 夜归临皋 · 夜饮东坡醒复醉
苏轼

夜饮东坡醒复醉，归来仿佛三更。家童鼻息已雷鸣。敲门都不应，倚杖听江声。

长恨此身非我有，何时忘却营营？夜阑风静縠纹平。小舟从此逝，江海寄余生。

Riverside Daffodils
Come Back LinnGao at Night
Su Shi

Drinking at Eastern Slope by night,
I sober, then get drunk again.
When I come back, it's near midnight,
I hear the thunder of my houseboy's snore;

I knock but no one answers the door.

What can I do but, leaning on my cane,

Listen to the river's refrain?

I long regret I am not master of my own.

When can I ignore the hums of up and down?

In the still night the soft winds quiver, On ripples of the river.

From now on I would vanish with my little boat;

For the rest of my life on the sea I would float.

关键词

refrain：副歌、迭歌、迭句。the river's refrain，对译"江声"。苏轼寓居临皋，在湖北黄县南长江边，故江声本为长江的涛声，译者以 refrain 译之，而未用 voice 等词，更为生动。

hums：繁忙。the hums of up and down，对译"营营（追求奔逐）"，直译为"浮浮沉沉的忙碌"。

float：漂浮。此句对译"江海寄余生"，float 一词将词人的飘零之意、超逸之意趣全盘托出。

译文

在东坡饮酒直至深夜，醉了睡，醒了又醉，回到家已是三更。家里的门童鼾声如雷。我怎么敲门都不应，只能挂着拐杖站在门外听江水滔滔之声。

只是感慨人在仕途身不由己，什么时候才能忘记这功名利禄？

夜尽风停江波平。好想乘舟告辞，从此隐匿江湖。

卜算子·不是爱风尘
严蕊

不是爱风尘，似被前缘误。花落花开自有时，总赖东君主。
去也终须去，住也如何住！若得山花插满头，莫问奴归处。

Song of Divination

Yan Rui

Is it a fallen life I love?

It's the mistake of fate above.

In time flowers blow, in time flowers fall;

It's all up to the east wind, all.

By fate! Have to go my way;

If not, where can I stay?

If my head were crowned with flowers,

Do not ask me where are my bowers!

关键词

in time：适时，本句对译"花落花开自有时"。译者将其拆成两个分句来翻译，两个 in time 对仗，更具节奏美，且调换了语序，先说花开再说花落，以使 fall 和 all 押韵。

bowers：凉亭、阴凉处，本句对译"莫问奴归处"，直译为"不要问我哪里是我的遮阴处"，意译为遮风挡雨的地方。

译文

不是我生性爱好风尘，只是因为旧时姻缘耽误终身。我身不由己，命运只能像花开花落一样，自有司春之神安排。

自然渴望脱离苦海，但现在也只能留在这里。若能有一日过上一般农妇的日子，也不必问我的归宿了。

严 蕊

　　严蕊，原姓周，字幼芳，南宋中期女词人。出身低微，自幼习乐礼诗书，后沦为台州营妓。学识渊博，诗词语意清新，四方闻名，时人有不远千里慕名相访者。词作多佚，现仅存《如梦令》《鹊桥仙》《卜算子》三首。

少年游·草·春风吹碧

高观国

春风吹碧，春云映绿，晓梦入芳裀。软衬飞花，远连流水，一望隔香尘。

萋萋多少江南恨，翻忆翠罗裙。冷落闲门，凄迷古道，烟雨正愁人。

Wandering While Young

Grass

Gao Guanguo

Greened by the breeze of spring,

Under clouds on the wing,

Your fragrant land seems like a morning dream.

As soft as fallen blooms, As far as water looms,

I stretch my eyes, we' re separated by a fragrant stream.

How much regret and grief on Southern shore

Remind me of the green silk skirt I adore.

Grass overgrown before her door

Near a pathway of yore,

The mist and water sadden me all the more.

关键词

loom：隐现。此句对译"远连流水"，远远地随着流水伸向天际，一个 loom 准确地勾勒出流水的辽远与曲折。

all the more：更加。此句对译"烟雨正愁人"，直译为"烟雨使我更为悲伤了"。more 还与下片的所有句尾词押韵，为译者炼字之成果，尽显音律美。

译文

春风吹绿了青草，在天上白云的映照下更显青翠。我在梦里进入了这芳草的世界。花瓣随风洒落，随流水远去。一眼望去，伊人的身影已被带着香气的尘烟阻隔。

葱郁的芳草留下了多少相思之苦，我回忆着脑海中的翠罗裙。冷落的闲庭，凄迷的古道，潇潇的烟雨让人愁。

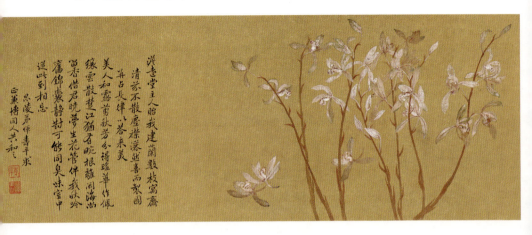

高观国

高观国，字宾王，号竹屋，山阴（今浙江绍兴）人。与史达祖友善，时常相互唱和，词亦齐名，时称"高史"。有词集《竹屋痴语》存世，词作句琢字炼，格律谨严，继承了周邦彦的风格，同时也受到"体制高雅"的姜夔词风的影响。

卜算子 · 黄州定慧院寓居作 · 缺月挂疏桐
苏轼

缺月挂疏桐，漏断人初静。谁见幽人独往来，缥缈孤鸿影。
惊起却回头，有恨无人省。拣尽寒枝不肯栖，寂寞沙洲冷。

Song of Divination

Write in DingHui Temple in Huangzhou

Su Shi

From a sparse plane tree hangs the waning moon;

The water clock is still and hushed is man.

Who sees a hermit pacing up and down alone?

Is it the shadow of a swan?

Startled, he turns his head.

With a grief none behold.

Looking all over, he won't perch on branches dead.

But on the lonely sandbank cold.

关键词

sparse plane tree: sparse 稀疏的，plane tree 悬铃木，对译"疏桐"。以西方熟知的、相对应的植物悬铃木来译梧桐，更易理解。

water clock: 滴漏。"漏"是中国古代的一种计时仪器，类似于西方的沙漏，故译者以 water clock 对译之。

swan: 原意天鹅，对译"鸿"。按照鸿在生物学上的术语翻译，应为 anser cygnoides，但译者选用了在西方文化中代表优雅、纯洁和忠诚的"swan"来表达作者惟愿脱离政治倾轧和物欲的感情，更能达到意象上的对等。

译文

弯弯的月亮悬挂在零落的梧桐树上，夜深了，人们都安静歇下。有谁见到幽居的人独来独往，像极了缥缈的孤鸿。

突然惊坐起回头看，心中的愁苦无人懂。就像那一只挑遍了寒枝也不肯栖息的鸟，甘愿在这冰冷的沙洲忍受寂寞。

虞美人·宜州见梅作·天涯也有江南信
黄庭坚

天涯也有江南信，梅破知春近。夜阑风细得香迟，不道晓来开遍向南枝。

玉台弄粉花应妒，飘到眉心住。平生个里愿杯深，去国十年老尽少年心。

The Beautiful Lady Yu
Mume Viewed in Yizhou Blossoms
Huang Tingjian

Message comes from the south to the end of the sky,
When mumes burst open, spring is nigh.
At dead of night the wind is slight, your fragrance late.
Who knows at dawn your branches bloom at southern gate?

You're envied by powder of the Terrace of Jade;

You waft amid the brows and will not fade.

All my life long I love you with wine cup in hand;

My young heart oldens ten years away from homeland.

关键词

dead of night: 深夜，对译"夜阑（夜将尽时）"，此处为意译，和后文的 slight(轻微的、少量的)押韵，读来颇有顿挫的节律之美。

envied by: 被羡慕，对译"应妒"，译者以被动句译主动句，不用嫉妒而用羡慕，使得 jade 和下文的 fade 得以押韵，主语 you 也得以突出。

译文

在宜州也能感受到春天的气息，梅花绽放就知春天要来了。夜晚清风里的香气时隐时现，早上醒来才知道向南的枝条上已开满了梅花。

女子对镜梳妆引来梅花嫉妒，花瓣飘落到她的额头上。以前看到这种场景便想喝上一杯。但离开朝廷的十年里，早已没有了这种少年兴致。

黄庭坚

黄庭坚，字鲁直，号山谷道人，洪州分宁（今江西九江市修水县）人，江西诗派开山之祖。与杜甫、陈师道、陈与义素有"一祖三宗"之称；与张耒、晁补之、秦观游学于苏轼门下，合称为"苏门四学士"。生前与苏轼齐名，时称"苏黄"。著有《山谷词》存世。

辑二

莫失莫忘

鹊桥仙·纤云弄巧
秦观

纤云弄巧，飞星传恨，银汉迢迢暗度。金风玉露一相逢，便胜却人间无数。

柔情似水，佳期如梦，忍顾鹊桥归路。两情若是久长时，又岂在朝朝暮暮。

Immortals at the Magpie Bridge
Qin Guan

Clouds float like works of art,
Stars shoot with grief at heart.
Across the Milky Way the Cowherd meets the Maid.
When Autumn's Golden Wind embraces Dew of Jade,
All the love scenes on earth, however many, fade.

Their tender love flows like a stream;

Their happy date seems but a dream.

How can they bear a separate homeward way?

If love between both sides can last for aye,

Why need they stay together night and day?

关键词

like works of art：像艺术品一样，对译纤云"弄巧"。"弄"字的拟人意味，在艺术品一词中也得到传达。art 还和下句的尾词 heart 押韵。

embrace：拥抱，欣然接受，对译金风玉露"一相逢"。秋风白露的相逢，是彼此的拥抱，牛郎织女的相会又何尝不是？

last for aye：持续到永远，对译"久长时"。last for aye、night and day，结构、音律精细雕琢；way, aye, day 三个词也押韵，节奏之美考究。

译文

秋云多变，流星传恨，牛郎织女在七夕渡天河相会。

秋风白露在秋天相遇，胜过了人间无数的儿女情长。

温柔情感如水，美好时光如梦，不忍回顾各自回鹊桥两头的路。

如果双方的感情是坚贞不渝的，又何必执着于朝夕相守。

江城子·西城杨柳弄春柔
秦观

西城杨柳弄春柔，动离忧，泪难收。犹记多情、曾为系归舟。碧野朱桥当日事，人不见，水空流。

韶华不为少年留，恨悠悠，几时休？飞絮落花时候、一登楼。便作春江都是泪，流不尽，许多愁。

Riverside Town

Qin Guan

West of the town the willows sway in the winds of spring.

Thinking of our parting would bring

To my eyes ever-flowing tears.

I still remember to the sympathetic tree

Her hand tied my returning boat for me

By the red bridge in the green field on that day.

But now she no longer appears, Though water still flows away.

The youthful days once gone will never come again;

My grief is endless. When, Will it come to an end then?

While willow catkins and falling flowers fly,

I mount the tower high.

Even if my tears turn into a stream in May,

Could it carry away, My grief growing each day?

关键词

sympathetic: 讨人喜欢的、可爱的。sympathetic tree, 补足"犹记多情"的宾语，以讨人喜爱的树代指多情的她，取其"象征义"之美，比起直接说人多情，更符合中国文化的含蓄美。

the youthful days: 年轻的日子，对译"韶华""少年"二词。美好的年华是不会为少年停下脚步的，一旦离去，终不复返。

carry away: 带走，对译"流不尽"。即使满江的春水都化作了眼泪，就能带走我这满怀的惆怅吗？以反问句对译陈述句，加重了语气和情绪的表达。

译文

西城的杨柳逗弄着春天的柔情，撩拨起我心中的愁情，眼泪止不住地流了下来。还记得当年你为我拴下归来的小舟。碧绿的原野、红色的小桥还是当年的模样，人却已不在，只有桥下的水孤独地流淌。

美好的年华不为少年停留，离别的苦恨什么时候才能消失？迎着飘落的飞絮，我登上楼台。即便满江的春水都化作我的眼泪，也流不尽我心中的忧愁。

江城子·乙卯正月二十日夜记梦·
十年生死两茫茫
苏轼

十年生死两茫茫，不思量，自难忘。千里孤坟，无处话凄凉。
纵使相逢应不识，尘满面，鬓如霜。
夜来幽梦忽还乡，小轩窗，正梳妆。相顾无言，惟有泪千行。
料得年年肠断处，明月夜，短松冈。

Riverside Town
A Dream on the Night of the 20th Day of the 1st Moon 1075
Su Shi

For the long years the living of the dead knows nought,
Though to my mind not brought, Could the dead be forgot?
Her lonely grave is far, a thousand miles away.

To whom can I my grief convey?

Revived even if she be, could she still know me?

My face is worn with care, And frosted is my hair.

Last night I dreamed of coming to my native place;

She was making up her face, Before her mirror with grace.

Each saw the other hushed, But from our eyes tears gushed.

Can I not be heart-broken when I am awoken

From her grave clad with pines, Where only the moon shines!

关键词

nought: 无，乌有。knows nought 对译"两茫茫"之生死两不知，"乌有"一用，凄凉感顿生。nought, brought, forgot 形成工整的押韵，与原文的"茫""忘"之押韵交相辉映。

could the dead be forgot: 对译"自难忘"。一个"自"字表达出强烈的思念之情，译文以反问句对译陈述句，以改变语气的方式将这肯定语气表达得淋漓尽致，避免了情态频度上的流失。

with grace: 优雅地，文雅地。此处为深化的译法，这一意象原文是没有的，译者故意加词，以达意美，且和前文的 place 押韵，以达音美。

译文

你我生死相别已经十年了，纵使我不日夜思念，可终究难相忘。你的孤坟远在千里，让我无处诉说心中的悲凉。即便相逢，只怕你也认不出我了。我的脸上已满是灰尘,头发已花白。

夜里做梦回到了家乡,只见你在窗前对镜梳妆。相对无言,泪水却止不住地流。料想那明月照着、矮松相伴的坟山,是你年年因思念我而柔肠寸断的地方。

水龙吟·次韵章质夫杨花词·似花还似非花

苏轼

　　似花还似非花，也无人惜从教坠。抛家傍路，思量却是，无情有思。萦损柔肠，困酣娇眼，欲开还闭。梦随风万里，寻郎去处，又还被、莺呼起。

　　不恨此花飞尽，恨西园、落红难缀。晓来雨过，遗踪何在？一池萍碎。春色三分，二分尘土，一分流水。细看来，不是杨花，点点是离人泪。

Water Dragon Chant

Su Shi

They seem to be but are not flowers;
None pity them when they fall down in showers.

Forsaking leafy home, By the roadside they roam.

I think they're fickle, but they've sorrow deep.

Their grief-o' erladen bowels tender, Like willow branches slender;

Their leaves like wistful eyes near shut with sleep,

About to open, yet soon closed again.

They dream of drifting with the wind for long,

Long miles to find their men, But are aroused by orioles' song.

Grieve not for willow catkins flown away,

But that in western garden fallen petals red

Can't be restored. When dawns the day

And rain is o' er, we cannot find their traces

But in a pond with duckweeds overspread.

Of Spring's three Graces, Two have gone with the roadside dust

And one with waves. But if you just

Take a close look, then you will never

Find willow down but tears of those who part,

Which drop by drop, Fall without stop.

关键词

fickle: 浮躁的、变化无常的。全句对译"无情有思",杨花看似变化无常,却自有它的深愁。

wistful eyes: 失意的、伤感的眼睛,对译"娇眼",即美人娇媚的眼睛,比喻柳叶。古人诗赋中常称初生的柳叶为柳眼。此处直

接点出了 their leaves like wistful eyes（它们的叶子像伤感的眼睛），
运用了深化之法。

duckweeds：浮萍。"一池萍碎"，苏轼自注"杨花落水为浮萍，
验之信然"，此处的浮萍显然指杨花，但译者将其浅化，不仅意似
且更简洁。

译文

杨花像花又不像花，无人怜惜任它飘落。柳絮坠离枝头却又沿
路散落，看似无情，却有恋家之思。柳叶愁思萦绕，像极了妇人迷
离的娇眼，半梦半醒。梦中随风行路，寻郎而去，却被黄莺啼声惊醒。

不遗憾杨花落尽，只恨西园满地落红，难再回春。清晨一阵风雨，
连落红的踪迹都找不到了。只留一池浮萍。若把这春色分为三份，
两份混入泥土，一份付诸流水，最后都渐渐消失。细细看来，那不
是杨花，是离人伤心的眼泪。

临江仙 · 梦后楼台高锁
晏几道

梦后楼台高锁，酒醒帘幕低垂。去年春恨却来时。落花人独立，微雨燕双飞。

记得小苹初见，两重心字罗衣。琵琶弦上说相思。当时明月在，曾照彩云归。

Riverside Daffodils
Yan Jidao

Awake from dreams, I find the locked tower high;
Sober from wine, I see the curtain hanging low.
As last year spring grief seems to grow.
Amid the falling blooms alone stand I;
In the fine rain a pair of swallows fly.

I still remember when I first saw pretty Ping,

In silken dress embroidered with two hearts in a ring,

Revealing lovesickness by touching pipa's string.

The moon shines bright just as last year;

It did see her like a cloud disappear.

关键词

spring grief: 春天的忧伤，对译"春恨"。"春恨"为伤春惜春之意，而非怨恨春天，故译者将其意译，未用 hate，而以 grief 译之。

seems to grow: 对译"却来时"，grow 一词用得很精妙，它本有生长、长成之意，好似这春天的忧伤像种子一般在心底生根发芽，且与 low 押韵。

amid: 四周是，被……所环绕。译者用了倒装句式，且以 amid 和 alone 一对反义词凸显出了"落花人独立"的具体情境，意境表达得完整准确。

fine rain: 对译"微雨"。fine 既和前半句的 falling 形成对仗；另者，fine 也有"美好""细微"两层含义，既译出了"细雨蒙蒙"之情态，又突出了"美好"的意境。

译文

深夜梦回发现楼台朱门紧闭，酒醒后见帘幕重重低垂。去年春天的愁绪在这时涌上心头。人在落花中独立，燕子在细雨中双飞。

记得与歌女初见时，她身穿两重心字香熏过的衣裳。轻弹琵琶诉说相思。当时明月今犹在，曾映照过她彩云般的身姿归去。

长相思·长相思

晏几道

长相思，长相思。若问相思甚了期，除非相见时。
长相思，长相思。欲把相思说似谁，浅情人不知。

Everlasting Longing

Yan Jidao

I yearn for long,

I yearn for long.

When may I end my yearning song?

Until you come along.

I yearn for long,

I yearn for long.

To whom may I sing my love song?

To none in love not strong.

关键词

yearning song：怀念的歌曲、诗歌，song 有押韵的诗歌之意，此句对译"若问相思甚了期"，若问这相思何时是尽头，直译为"我何时能写完这怀念之词"。

strong：此处取"坚强的、强烈的"之意，前加 not，即不深情、不强烈，对译"浅情人（薄情寡义之人）"。

译文

长久的相思，长久的相思，要问这相思何时了，直到相见之时。

长久的相思，长久的相思，想把这相思说给谁听，薄情之人是不能体会到的。

卜算子·我住长江头
李之仪

我住长江头，君住长江尾。日日思君不见君，共饮长江水。
此水几时休，此恨何时已。只愿君心似我心，定不负相思意。

Song of Divination
Li Zhiyi

I live upstream and you downstream.

From night to night of you I dream.

Unlike the stream you're not in view,

Though we both drink from River Blue.

Where will the water no more flow?

When will my grief no longer grow?

1 wish your heart would be like mine.

Then not in vain for you I pine.

关键词

blue：蓝色的、忧郁的。此句对译"共饮长江水"，译者加了 blue 一词修饰 River，一是以 blue 的双关义表达词人的思念与叹息，二是将此句凑足了七个音节，与前半句对仗工整。

no more flow：对译"几时休"，译者采用了 no more 的否定表达，保持了中英文句式上对偶的稳定，且英文用否定词更能增强思念的感情。

译文

我住在长江源头，君住在长江尽头。我日日思念却无法相见，只能共饮这长江之水。

江水何时枯竭，离别之恨何时才能停止。只希望君心如我这般坚定，定不辜负这番情意。

李之仪

　　李之仪，字端叔，自号姑溪居士、姑溪老农，沧州无棣（今属山东）人。北宋中后期"苏门"文人集团重要成员，一生官职虽不显赫，但其与苏轼的文缘情谊却令人称道。其词多清新婉丽，长调近柳永，小令近秦观。著有《姑溪词》《姑溪居士前集》和《姑溪题跋》。

蝶恋花 · 槛菊愁烟兰泣露
晏殊

槛菊愁烟兰泣露，罗幕轻寒，燕子双飞去。明月不谙离恨苦，斜光到晓穿朱户。

昨夜西风凋碧树，独上高楼，望尽天涯路。欲寄彩笺兼尺素。山长水阔知何处？

Butterflies in Love with Flowers

Yan Shu

Orchids shed tears with doleful asters in mist grey.

How can they stand the cold silk curtains can't allay?

A pair of swallows flies away.

The moon, which knows not parting grief, sheds slanting light,

Through crimson windows all the night.

Last night the western breeze

Blew withered leaves off trees.

I mount the tower high, And strain my longing eye.

I'll send a message to my dear,

But endless ranges and streams separate us far and near.

关键词

allay：减轻，使缓和，尤指情绪的减轻。此处指燕子不耐罗幕轻寒飞去，实际词人是以燕子说人，故译者用了 can't allay，点明词人心理上孤子凄清的寒意无法减轻。

crimson windows：深红色的窗户，对译"朱户"。朱户，犹言朱门，指大户人家。此处译者为便于理解，未译作大户，而直接等化译之。

strain：竭力，使劲。strain my longing eye，对译"望尽天涯路"，此处为意译，直译为"我渴望的眼睛已经竭尽全力了"，对"尽"字的阐释十分到位。

译文

栏外的菊花被愁烟笼罩，兰花上的露珠像眼泪晶莹，帷幕外微寒，一双燕子飞过。明月当空，不知离别的苦恨，月光直到破晓还斜洒在窗内。

昨夜的西风吹落了树上的叶子。我独自上高楼，看到那天地的尽头。想寄一封彩色的信笺给心上人，又不知他在这天地间的何处。

相思令·蘋满溪
张先

蘋满溪，柳绕堤。相送行人溪水西，回时陇月低。
烟霏霏，风凄凄。重倚朱门听马嘶，寒鸥相对飞。

Song of Longing
Zhang Xian

Duckweeds float on the brook in view;
The bank flanked with willow trees.
West of the brook I bade my lord adieu;
Back, I see the waning moon freeze.

Veiled in mist grey
And dreary breeze,

Leaning again on the door,I hear the horse neigh,

And see the gulls white two by two in flight.

关键词

freeze：冻住，突然停住。the waning moon freeze，对译"陇月低"，低垂的山间明月，直译为"残月冻结"，更显凄清。

veiled：遮掩，全句直译为"掩盖在灰雾之中"，对译"烟霏霏（烟很盛的样子）"。原词客观描述环境，译文加入动词 veiled，摹状，读来更有代入感。

译文

绿萍铺满了小溪，柳树的枝条在岸堤上飘动。沿着溪畔送行人西行，折返时已见明月低挂山间。

烟雨霏霏，寒风凄凄。依靠着朱门向远处看去，只听见过路的马儿嘶鸣，天边的寒鸥飞来飞去。

张 先

　　张先，字子野，乌程（今浙江湖州）人，北宋婉约派词家代表人物，曾因三处善用"影"字，人称"张三影"。"能诗及乐府，至老不衰"，语言工巧，其词内容大多反映士大夫的诗酒生活和男女之情，对都市社会生活也有所体现。

诉衷情 · 花前月下暂相逢
张先

花前月下暂相逢。苦恨阻从容。何况酒醒梦断，花谢月朦胧。
花不尽，月无穷。两心同。此时愿作，杨柳千丝，绊惹春风。

Telling Innermost Feeling
Zhang Xian

Before flowers, beneath the moon, shortly we met
Only to part with bitter regret.
What's more, I wake from wine and dreams
To find fallen flowers and dim moonbeams.

Flowers will bloom again; The moon will wax and wane.
Would our hearts be the same?

I'd turn the flame, Of my heart, string on string,

Into willow twigs to retain, the breeze of spring.

关键词

wax and wane：月圆月缺、盈亏，对译"月无穷"，花月意象所呈现的均是时光的流转，词人情感精神所经历的曲折变化也得以凸现。

turn the flame：打开强烈的情感，对译"愿作"，译文未用would like to 等寻常之语，特选用 flame 一词极言意愿之强烈。

string on string：一串接一串的，对译杨柳"千丝"，"千"在此为概数，言其多，译文用 string on string 摹状，从数量和形态上看都很准确。

译文

恋人在花前月下短暂相约后，便要分离。深恨那些拆散我们的理由。酒醒之后，美梦断了，花儿谢了，连月亮都失去了光亮。

花开不败，月盈而亏。我们两人的心永远在一起。此时，我愿成为一棵柳树，这样就能一直和春风牵缠了。

蝶恋花·庭院深深深几许

欧阳修

庭院深深深几许，杨柳堆烟，帘幕无重数。玉勒雕鞍游冶处，楼高不见章台路。

雨横风狂三月暮，门掩黄昏，无计留春住。泪眼问花花不语，乱红飞过秋千去。

Butterflies in Love with Flowers

Ouyang Xiu

Deep, deep the courtyard where he is, so deep
It's veiled by smokelike willows heap on heap,
By curtain on curtain and screen on screen.
Leaving his saddle and bridle, there he has been
Merry-making.From my tower his trace can't be seen.

The third moon now, the wind and rain are raging late;

At dusk I bar the gate,

But I can't bar in spring.

My tearful eyes ask flowers, but they fail to bring

An answer, I see red blooms fly over the swing.

关键词

smokelike：烟状的。此句对译"杨柳堆烟"，"堆烟"是形容杨柳浓密，译者以 smokelike 等化译之，意境表达得更为具体可感。

Merry-making：狂欢。章台为汉长安街名，后以章台特指歌妓聚居之地。译者加词深化，以 Merry-making 道出章台一词的典故。

译文

庭院深深，不见底。杨柳依依，烟云重重，眼前像蒙住了一层轻纱。豪华的车马停驻在烟街柳巷，家中女子登上高楼也见不到通往章台的道路。

风雨交加的暮春三月，即使用大门将黄昏景色关起，也无法阻止春归去。女子泪眼婆娑问落花，落花默默无语，花瓣被春风纷乱地吹起，零零落落飞到了秋千外。

欧阳修

　　欧阳修，字永叔，号醉翁，晚号六一居士，庐陵（今江西吉安）人。
与韩愈、柳宗元、苏轼、苏洵、苏辙、王安石、曾巩合称"唐宋八
大家"，并与韩愈、柳宗元、苏轼合称"千古文章四大家"，是宋
代文学史上最早开创一代文风的文坛领袖，并领导了北宋诗文革新
运动，继承发展了韩愈的古文理论。曾主修《新唐书》，并独撰《新
五代史》，有《欧阳文忠集》传世。

生查子·药名闺情·相思意已深
陈亚

相思意已深，白纸书难足。字字苦参商，故要檀郎读。
分明记得约当归，远至樱桃熟。何事菊花时，犹未回乡曲？

Mountain Hawthorn
Chen Ya

I am so deep in love,
Paper's not long enough.
I'm grieved from you to part.
Why don't you know my heart?

You've promised to come back
Before ripen cherries black.

Chrysanthemums now bloom.

Why are you not in our room?

关键词

grieved：悲伤的。此句中"参商"指参、商二星，参星在西，商星（即辰星）在东，此出彼没，永不相见，比喻双方隔绝。译者未译"参商"，而直译为"我悲伤于你我的分别"，为浅化译法，但意思准确。

ripen：使成熟。此句对译"远至樱桃熟"，直译为"在樱桃成熟变红之前"。"樱桃"本为中医药材名，原词以"樱桃成熟"对应时间，译者则等化译之。

译文

自与夫君离别以来，我的思念日渐加深，这短短的信笺不足以让我倾诉。信中的每个字都让我想起我们天各一方，希望夫君仔细阅读。

我清楚记得你的归期，说最迟也是樱桃成熟时。为什么到了菊花开放时，还没有听到你的消息呢？

陈　亚

　　陈亚，字亚之，维扬（今江苏扬州）人。好以药名为诗词，有药名诗百首，其中佳句如"风月前湖夜，轩窗半夏凉"，颇为人所称道，药名词如《生查子》，称道者亦多。著有《澄原集》《陈亚之文集》，已佚。

长相思·吴山青
林逋

吴山青，越山青。两岸青山相送迎，谁知离别情？
君泪盈，妾泪盈。罗带同心结未成，江头潮已平。

The Everlasting Longing
Lin Bu

Northern hills green,

Southern hills green,

The green hills greet your ship sailing between.

Who knows my parting sorrow keen?

Tears from your eyes,

Tears from my eyes,

Could silken girdle strengthen our hear-to-heart ties?

O see the river rise?

关键词

Northern hills：对译"吴山"。"吴山"在此泛指钱塘江北岸的群山，古属吴国，故译者以 Northern hills（北山）对译之，也与下文的 Southern hills（南山，此处指越山，钱塘江南岸的群山，古属越国）相对。

keen：强烈的。译者加 keen 一词修饰 my parting sorrow（离别的悲伤），表达了原词的离愁之深，也凑了韵，keen 一词与上片尾词均押韵。

译文

青翠的吴山和越山，两岸相对，隔江相映，仿佛在迎送往来的过客。可它们哪里懂人间的离愁别绪呢？

你泪眼盈盈，我泪眼盈盈，你我定了情却不能在一起。江潮过后水面已经恢复平静了，我也要扬帆远行了。

林 逋

　　林逋，字君复，后世称和靖先生，奉化大里（今浙江宁波）人，北宋著名隐逸诗人。性孤高自好，喜恬淡，曾漫游江淮间，后隐居西湖孤山，终生不仕不娶，唯喜植梅养鹤，自谓"以梅为妻，以鹤为子"，人称"梅妻鹤子"。

青玉案 · 凌波不过横塘路
贺铸

凌波不过横塘路。但目送、芳尘去。锦瑟华年谁与度？月桥花院，琐窗朱户，只有春知处。

飞云冉冉蘅皋暮，彩笔新题断肠句。若问闲情都几许？一川烟草，满城风絮，梅子黄时雨。

Green Jade Cup
He Zhu

Never again will she tread on the lakeside lane.

I follow with my eyes

The fragrant dusts that rise.

With whom is she now spending her delightful hours,

Playing on zither string,

On a crescent-shaped bridge, in a yard full of flowers,

Or in a vermeil bower only known to spring?

At dusk the floating cloud leaves the grass-fragrant plain;

With blooming brush I write heart-broken verse again.

If you ask me how deep and wide I am lovesick,

Just see a misty plain where grass grows thick,

A townful of willow down wafting on the breeze,

Or drizzling rain yellowing all mume-trees!

关键词

delightful hours：令人愉悦的、宜人的时光，对译"锦瑟年华（美好的青春时期）"。此句直译为"正是青春年华时候，可什么人能与她一起欢度？"

the grass-fragrant plain：长着香草的平原，对译"蘅皋（长着香草的沼泽中的高地）"。译者以 grass-fragrant 概指杜蘅这类香草。

yellowing：名词作动词，使变黄。此句对译"梅子黄时雨"，直译为"毛毛细雨染黄了所有的梅子树"。

译文

轻盈的脚步匆匆走过横塘，我只能目送她像芳尘一样远去。她的青春年华与谁一起度过？筑拱桥花满园，锁纹窗朱红门，只有春天才知道她的住处。

天上的云快速飞过，小洲在长着香草的沼泽中若隐若现，我用新笔书写新愁。要问我情愁有多少？就像这平原上的烟草，满城飘飞的柳絮，梅子成熟时的细雨。

蝶恋花·伫倚危楼风细细
柳永

伫倚危楼风细细，望极春愁，黯黯生天际。草色烟光残照里，无言谁会凭阑意？

拟把疏狂图一醉，对酒当歌，强乐还无味。衣带渐宽终不悔，为伊消得人憔悴。

Butterflies in Love with Flowers
Liu Yong

I lean alone on balcony in light, light breeze;
As far as the eye sees,
On the horizon dark parting grief grows unseen.
In fading sunlight rises smoke over grass green.
Who understands why mutely on the rails I lean?

l'd drown in wine my parting grief;

Chanting before the cup, strained mirth brings no relief.

I find my gown too large, but I will not regret;

It's worth while growing languid for my coquette.

关键词

light, light breeze: 对译"风细细"，细细的风自然很轻，词人的丝丝惆怅、绵绵情意尽显。译文与原词音节对应，意境相同。

parting grief grows unseen: 此短语为译者加词增译，将"愁"具化为离别的伤感。grows 表示忧愁的产生，将其拟人化，更能展现原词的用词优美，"unseen"则解释了忧愁并非真的生在天际，而是词人心中所想。

mutely: 缄默的，对译"无言"，贴切地展现了词人因伤感而无言的意境，译者选词精准，别有匠心。

lean: 倚靠。慢词长调是柳永词的一大特点，故译者用了breeze, sees, unseen, green, lean 等有长音的词，体现了译文的"音美"。

chant: 反复地唱歌、吟咏、说话。

mirth: 欢乐，在古英语中与喝酒欢乐有关，译者选词考究，找到了英汉词汇互通之处。该句直译为"勉强的欢乐并不能缓解（春愁）"。

languid: 苦思，因渴望而变得憔悴，对译"憔悴"。

译文

　　我久倚在高楼的栏杆上，任凭丝丝春风拂面。望不尽的春愁，沮丧的心情从遥远的天际弥漫而来。飘忽缭绕的云霭雾气将青绿的草淹没在夕阳里，谁能理解我独自靠在栏杆上的沉默。

　　本打算狂放不羁地醉一场，却不料在笙歌里举杯时，又深感这样勉强寻乐反而索然无味。我因思念日渐消瘦也不会后悔，宁愿为她消瘦得神色憔悴。

柳 永

柳永，原名三变，字景庄，后改字耆卿，因在家族兄弟中排行第七，时人又称其柳七，福建崇安（今福建武夷山）人，婉约派代表词人。其词有雅俚二类，长于铺叙，工于写景言情，讲究章法结构，富于音乐美。著有《乐章集》。

雨霖铃·寒蝉凄切

柳永

寒蝉凄切，对长亭晚，骤雨初歇。

都门帐饮无绪，留恋处，兰舟催发。

执手相看泪眼，竟无语凝噎。

念去去，千里烟波，暮霭沉沉楚天阔。

多情自古伤离别，更那堪，冷落清秋节！

今宵酒醒何处？杨柳岸、晓风残月。

此去经年，应是良辰好景虚设。

便纵有、千种风情，更与何人说？

Bells Ringing in the Rain
Liu Yong

Cicadas chill

Drearily shrill.

We stand face to face in an evening hour

Before the pavilion, after a sudden shower.

Can we care for drinking before we part?

At the city gate

We are lingering late,

But the boat is waiting for me to depart.

Hand in hand we gaze at each other's tearful eyes

And burst into sobs with words congealed on our lips.

I'll go my way,

Far, far away.

On miles and miles of misty waves where sail ships,

And evening clouds hang low in boundless Southern skies.

Lovers would grieve at parting as of old.

How could I stand this clear autumn day so cold!

Where shall I be found at daybreak

From wine awake?

Moored by a riverbank planted with willow trees

Beneath the waning moon and in the morning breeze.

I'll be gone for a year.

In vain would good times and fine scenes appear.

However gallant I am on my part,

To whom can I lay bare my heart?

关键词

chill：寒冷、寒意，与 shrill（尖锐的）用了双声叠韵的修辞，对译"寒蝉凄切"，此处为等化的翻译手法。drearily（沉寂的、可怕的）深化修饰蝉鸣，表达出深秋的荒凉之感，也让离别更为悲凉。

Southern skies：对译"楚天"，此处的"楚天"并非楚国的天空，而是指南方的天空，故译者将其浅化译之。

lay bare：袒露、显露。此句对译"更与何人说"，直译为"我能向谁袒露心迹呢"，深沉的无奈感顿生。译者以倒装句式翻译，做到了句尾 part 与 heart 的押韵。

译文

秋蝉的叫声凄凉急促，傍晚时分，暴雨骤停，我在这长亭设帐饯行，却没有畅饮的心情。还在依依不舍，船上的人已经开始催促。握着对方的手，泪眼婆娑，千言万语噎在喉咙说不出来。这一路远去，千里烟波浩渺，低沉的云霞笼罩南天，深厚广阔，不知尽头。

自古以来，多情的人总为离别感伤，更何况是在这清冷的秋天。谁知我今夜酒醒时身在何处？只剩岸边杨柳、晨风和残月陪我。此去一别多年，这么好的景色也形同虚设。就算有千万心绪，又能跟谁去说呢？

醉花阴 · 薄雾浓云愁永昼
李清照

薄雾浓云愁永昼，瑞脑消金兽。佳节又重阳，玉枕纱厨，半夜凉初透。

东篱把酒黄昏后，有暗香盈袖。莫道不销魂？帘卷西风，人比黄花瘦。

Tipsy in the Flowers' Shade
Li Qingzhao

Veiled in thin mist and thick cloud, how sad the long day!
Incense from golden censer melts away.
The Double Ninth comes again; Alone I still remain
In silken bed curtain, on pillow smooth like jade.
Feeling the midnight chill invade.

At dusk I drink before chrysanthemums in bloom,

My sleeves filled with fragrance and gloom. Say not my soul

Is not consumed. Should the west wind uproll

The curtain of my bower,

You'll see a face thinner than yellow flower.

关键词

melts away: 消失、融掉。此句对译"瑞脑消金兽",龙脑香在金兽香炉中缭袅,译者以 melts away 对译"消",不仅押韵,也十分准确。

alone: 孤独。alone I still remain,实为译者增补的内容,将表情感的词 alone 提前,以倒装句译之,强调词人因孤独而伤怀的情感,与上文的 sad 形成呼应。

uproll: 向上滚动,此句对译"帘卷西风"——西风乍起,卷帘而入,故译者将语序做了调整,实为西风卷帘。

face: 脸,此处指代"人",此句对译"人比黄花瘦"。译者用了英语中最常见的"提喻"的修辞手法,即以部分代替整体。

译文

薄雾浓云,愁绪无休止,焚香的冰片的烟雾在香炉中缭绕。又到了重阳佳节,睡在玉枕轻纱帐内,到了半夜才彻底凉快。

黄昏后,在东篱旁把酒赏菊,幽幽暗香盈满衣袖。别说清秋不让人伤神,待到西风吹起珠帘,人比那黄花更加消瘦。

一剪梅·红藕香残玉簟秋

李清照

红藕香残玉簟秋。轻解罗裳，独上兰舟。云中谁寄锦书来？雁字回时，月满西楼。

花自飘零水自流。一种相思，两处闲愁。此情无计可消除，才下眉头，却上心头。

A Twig of Mume Blossoms

Li Qingzhao

Fragrant lotus blooms fade, autumn chills mat of jade.

My silk robe doffed, I float alone in orchid boat.

Who in the cloud would bring me letters in brocade?

When swans come back in flight,

My bower is steeped in moonlight.

As fallen flowers drift and water runs its way,

One longing leaves no traces

But overflows two places.

O how can such lovesickness be driven away?

From eyebrows kept apart, Again it gnaws my heart.

关键词

mat：小地毯、垫子。mat of jade，对译"玉簟"，即精美的凉席。此句译者加了 chill（使寒冷）一词，直译为"荷花香润，秋寒玉席"。将原词暗含的青春易逝、"人去席冷"之意境尽数表达了出来。

in flight：在飞行中。此句对译"雁字回时"，come back in flight 强调了词人遥望云空，见大雁群归的当下，想到大雁传书，惦念游子行踪之情。flight 也与 moonlight 押了尾韵。

leaves no traces：没有留下任何痕迹。此句直译为"一种相思虽无痕迹，实则泛滥两处"，这是有情人的心灵感应，词人夫妇情笃爱深，相思却又不能相见的无奈思绪得以完美译出。

lovesickness：相思病。译者以相思译"此情"，为深化之法，将这情感点明。

译文

粉红色的荷花已经凋谢，光滑似玉的竹席传递着秋天的凉意。脱掉外衣，独自登上小船。谁的书信会穿过云层远寄而来？远去的大雁再飞回来时，已是月满之时，而月光也早就洒满了西楼。

　　落花独自飘零，溪水独自流淌。彼此相思，各挂心头。这种愁苦无法排解，才展开蹙眉，心里又忍不住开始挂念。

望江南 · 三月暮
吴文英

三月暮，花落更情浓。人去秋千闲挂月，马停杨柳倦嘶风。堤畔画船空。

恹恹醉，长日小帘栊。宿燕夜归银烛外，啼莺声在绿阴中。无处觅残红。

Dreaming of the South

Wu Wenying

Late in spring, The fallen blooms add to my growing gloom.

She's gone; the crescent moon hangs idle over the swing;

The horse beneath willow trees

Neighs tiredly in the breeze.

By waterside an empty painted boat is tied.

Drunk and weary,

All the day long I stay behind the curtain dreary.

The swallows coming back at night

Take rest beyond my silver candlelight

Orioles' warble fades amid green shades.

Nowhere out of the bower, Can be found an unfallen flower.

关键词

add to: 增加。add to my growing gloom, 对译"更情浓"，直译为"使我日益增长的忧郁更为增加了"，译者以 add to, growing 极言 gloom（忧郁）之深。

weary: 疲惫的、疲倦的，对译"恹恹（精神不振貌）"，译者将其浅化译之，且调换了"恹恹"和"醉"的顺序，让 weary 不仅是一个修饰词，更以一个连接词 and, 强调了 drunk 和 weary 的因果关系。

译文

三月暮春，花儿凋落，情反而更浓。人离开后，秋千在月下孤单地挂着，就连拴在柳树下的马儿也懒得迎风嘶叫。而堤边的画船上更是空无一人。

春困袭来昏昏欲睡，珠帘长日低垂。夜晚燕子归来却因银烛不敢归巢，绿荫中流莺啼啭。春光流逝，连那凋落的花红也无处可寻。

吴文英

　　吴文英，字君特，号梦窗，晚年又号觉翁，四明（今浙江宁波）人。一生未仕，游幕终老。词风幽隐密丽，注重音律，精于炼字。著有《梦窗词》，存词三百四十余首。

风入松 · 听风听雨过清明
吴文英

听风听雨过清明，愁草瘗花铭。楼前绿暗分携路，一丝柳、一寸柔情。料峭春寒中酒，交加晓梦啼莺。

西园日日扫林亭，依旧赏新晴。黄蜂频扑秋千索，有当时、纤手香凝。惆怅双鸳不到，幽阶一夜苔生。

Wind through Pines
Wu Wenying

Hearing the wind and rain while mourning for the dead,
Sadly I draft an elegy on flowers.
Over dark green lane hang willow twigs like thread,
We parted before the bowers.
Each twig revealing, Our tender feeling.

I drown my grief in wine in chilly spring;

Drowsy,I wake again when orioles sing.

In West Garden I sweep the pathway

From day to day, Enjoying the fine view, Still without you.

On the ropes of the swing the wasps often alight

For fragrance spread by fingers fair.

I'm grieved not to see your foot traces, all night

The mossy steps are left untrodden there.

关键词

revealing: 展现。此句对译"一丝柳、一寸柔情",直译为"每一根嫩枝都透出我们的柔情"。

drowsy: 困倦的。"交加"在此形容杂乱,本是酒后困倦无比,不料又被啼莺唤醒,译者未直译"交加"一词,而以 drowsy 点明了当时困倦的状态。

untrodden: 未受践踏的,折回,对应前文的 your foot traces(你的足迹)。此句对译"幽阶一夜苔生",直译为"那长满青苔的台阶无人踏足"。

译文

清明时节风雨声声,我为落花感伤,将它们安葬并草拟了一篇碑铭。当年与故人分别的小楼前绿柳成荫,每一条摇曳的柳丝都寄托了我的柔情。我在微凉的春日饮醉了酒,清晨黄莺的啼声惊扰了我的梦。

　　我每天都会把西园的亭台和树林洒扫干净，在雨过新晴后我依然会去游园赏春。黄蜂飞舞着扑向秋千的绳索，这里仍存留着当年佳人手握时留下的芳香。想到这里，我不禁惆怅再也看不到穿着鸳鸯绣鞋的佳人前来，一夜间青苔黯然长满了幽深的台阶。

浣溪沙·门隔花深梦旧游
吴文英

门隔花深梦旧游，夕阳无语燕归愁。玉纤香动小帘钩。
落絮无声春堕泪，行云有影月含羞。东风临夜冷于秋。

Silk-washing Stream
Wu Wenying

I dreamed of the door parting me from my dear flower,
The setting sun was mute and homing swallows drear.
Her fair hands hooked up fragrant curtains of her bower.

The willow down falls silently and spring sheds tear;
The floating clouds cast shadows when the moon feels shy;
The spring wind blows at night colder than autumn high.

关键词

fair hands：美丽的手，对译"玉纤"，纤细如玉的指头，多指美人的手。故译者浅化译为"她的美丽的手"。

cast shadows：投影。译者加了动词 cast，将"行云有影"的客观化为主观，拟人化的手法展现出原词"表面写自然，实则写情"的妙处。

译文

梦境中我回到了旧时的庭院，簌簌繁花将院门遮掩，斜阳静默无语，归巢的燕子似乎也带着忧愁。她的纤纤玉手带着幽香，轻轻将幕帘从帘钩上放下。

轻柔的柳絮悄无声息地飘落，仿佛是春天伤感流下的眼泪，月亮像害羞的女子般躲在浮云后投下云翳。料峭的东风吹过，清冷得仿佛秋天一般。

夜合花·自鹤江入京泊葑门外有感·柳暝河桥
吴文英

柳暝河桥，莺晴台苑，短策频惹春香。当时夜泊，温柔便入深乡。词韵窄，酒杯长。翦蜡花、壶箭催忙。共追游处，凌波翠陌，连棹横塘。

十年一梦凄凉。似西湖燕去，吴馆巢荒。重来万感，依前唤酒银罂。溪雨急，岸花狂。趁残鸦、飞过苍茫。故人楼上，凭谁指与，芳草斜阳。

Night Flower
Wu Wenying

The bridge O'er shadowed by a willow tree,
Orioles warbling over sunny bowers,
Our ride was often sweetened by spring flowers.

When our boat in delight

Was moored at night,

My tender love went deep into the land with me.

We wrote verse line,

Long we drank wine,

And trimmed lamp wick:

Time passed so quick.

Can I forget our land or river trip

By rowing boat or flipping whip?

Like dreary dreams ten years have passed.

The swallows have flown over the Lake of the West,

Leaving in ancient palace but an empty nest.

I feel so sad and drear

When again I come here.

I call for silver cups of wine as before;

Over the brook the rain comes fast

And falling petals run riot on the shore,

E'en the lingering crows fly across the sky vast.

In the bower where lived my dear, alas!

Who'd grieve at sunset over fragrant grass!

关键词

verse line：诗行，对译"词韵"。词韵，在此指词致气韵，是
词人以当日的词才笨拙反衬共饮清觞、共剪灯花的陶醉。译者以诗

行代指，契合词人的身份，明白晓畅，又与下文的 wine 凑了韵。

　　grieve at：对……感到悲伤，译者加词深化，此句对译"凭谁指与，芳草斜阳"，直译为"谁会（与我一起）伤感于芳草斜阳"。

译文

　　日暮时，杨柳掩映着河桥；晴日里，黄莺在台苑上鸣啭。多少次，我曾与你策马同赏这春光。还记得那一回夜泊此地，你我温柔相拥进入梦乡。诗词句短，酒味绵长。蜡烛燃烧得快，需要不停剪芯，壶漏中的箭筹时刻提醒着我时光飞逝。与你共游之处，青翠的小路留下你轻盈的脚步，小船穿过一个接一个的池塘。

　　十年如梦，醒后倍感凄凉。就好像人去楼空，燕去巢荒。如今我重到蓟门，百感交集，像从前一样唤酒品尝。小雨密集，岸上落花轻狂。几只寒鸦飞过这苍茫的天空。来到这故人楼宇，还有谁陪我凭栏远眺，看这芳草斜阳。

钗头凤·红酥手

陆游

红酥手，黄縢酒，满城春色宫墙柳。东风恶，欢情薄。一怀愁绪，几年离索。错，错，错！

春如旧，人空瘦，泪痕红浥鲛绡透。桃花落，闲池阁。山盟虽在，锦书难托。莫，莫，莫！

Phoenix Hairpin

Lu You

Pink hands so fine, Gold-branded wine,

Spring paints the willows green palace walls can't confine.

East wind unfair, Happy times rare.

In my heart sad thoughts throng; We've been separated for years long.

Wrong, wrong, wrong!

Spring is as green, In vain she's lean.

Her kerchief soaked with tears and red with stains unclean.

Peach blossoms fall, Near deserted hall.

Our oath is still there. Lo! No word to her can go.

No, no, no!

关键词

paints：绘画、染色，全句直译为"春天将垂柳染绿"，一个动词将满城春色描绘得更生动。

can't confine：不能限制。全句直译为"宫墙也限制不了它们"，将原词春意盎然的意境传达给了读者，衬托出词人的喜悦之情。

east wind unfair：对译"东风恶"，译文保留了 east wind（东风）这一意象，因为在英文中东风即寒冷之风，和原词的内涵大致吻合。且译者以 unfair（不公平）对译"恶"，将陆母拆散他们的恶意之举描写得绘声绘色，也和下文的 rare 押韵。

throng：聚集。sad thoughts throng，全句对译"一怀愁绪"，直译为"愁绪郁结"。throng 一词为神来之笔，词人强烈的离别之苦准确形象地得以传达。

译文

粉嫩酥软的手里，端着装满黄滕酒的酒杯，满城春色，你像宫墙里的绿柳让人无法触及。春风多可恶，吹散了欢愉，让人情淡薄。

酒杯里都是愁绪，离群索居的日子让人愁苦。只能感叹：错，错，错！

春日的景色依旧，人却因相思消瘦。泪水湿润了脸上的胭脂，湿透了手帕。桃花飘落，楼阁空荡。曾经的誓言仍在，可锦书却再也不能交到你手上。只能感叹：莫，莫，莫！

钗头凤·世情薄
唐琬

世情薄，人情恶，雨送黄昏花易落。晓风干，泪痕残。欲笺心事，独语斜阑。难，难，难！

人成各，今非昨，病魂常似秋千索。角声寒，夜阑珊。怕人寻问，咽泪装欢。瞒，瞒，瞒！

Phoenix Hairpin

Tang Wan

The world unfair, True manhood rare.

Dusk melts away in rain and blooming trees turn bare.

Morning wind high, Tear traces dry.

I'd write to him what's in my heart; Leaning on rails, I speak apart.

Hard, hard, hard!

Go each our ways! Gone are our days.

My sick soul groans like ropes of swing which sways.

The horn blows cold; Night has grown old.

Afraid my grief may be descried, I try to hide my tears undried.

Hide, hide, hide!

关键词

the world unfair, true manhood rare: 对译"世情薄""人情恶"，皆为三个单词（四个音节），且中心词和修饰词的位置也一致，同原词一样，对仗十分工整，做到了"形美"。

melt away: 融化，消逝。对译雨"送"黄昏，直译为"黄昏在雨中消逝"。

the horn blows cold, night has grown old: 对译"角声寒""夜阑珊"，皆为四个单词（四个音节），且译者将 cold 和 old 后置，不仅对仗工整，且押韵。全词译文为译者"三美论"实践之典范。

译文

世间薄情，人情险恶，黄昏落雨，花瓣满地。晨风吹干眼泪，脸上残留泪痕。想要写下心事，却只能倚着斜栏自言自语。怎么这么难！

人单影只，今非昔比，积劳成疾，久病缠身。远方角声孤寒，我似这夜衰残。害怕别人关心，只能咽下眼泪强颜欢笑。心事只得瞒，瞒，瞒！

唐 琬

唐琬，字蕙仙，越州山阴（今浙江绍兴）人。陆游原配，不见容于陆母，被逼令休弃。数年后，陆游游览沈园，与其不期而遇，在壁上题写一阕《钗头凤》，写罢，搁笔而去。沈园重逢后，唐琬悲恸不已，回家后反复玩味陆游的题词，便和了一首同样曲牌的词，不久便郁郁而卒。

辑三

寻山

踏海

西江月·夜行黄沙道中·明月别枝惊鹊
辛弃疾

明月别枝惊鹊，清风半夜鸣蝉。稻花香里说丰年，听取蛙声一片。

七八个星天外，两三点雨山前。旧时茅店社林边，路转溪桥忽见。

The Moon over the West River
Xin Qiji

Startled by magpies leaving the branch in moonlight,
I hear cicadas shrill in the breeze at midnight.
The ricefields' sweet smell promises a bumper year;
Listen, how frogs' croaks please the ear!

Beyond the clouds seven or eight stars twinkle;

Before the hills two or three raindrops sprinkle.

There is an inn beside the village temple. Look!

The winding path leads to the hut beside the brook.

关键词

promise a bumper year：对译"说丰年"，直译为"稻香许下了丰年"。promise，承诺、许下，把这丰年的依据说得更为明白。

please the ear：让耳朵开心、满意。此处为意译，补足原词省略的主语，强调了 listen 的结果和当时愉悦的心情。ear 和 year 结尾押韵，两句对仗工整，且全词英译均如此，完美再现了原文的对仗押韵，体现了译者的"韵体翻译法"。

the winding path：曲径，对译"路转"，以名词表达了动词之意。

译文

明月爬上树梢，惊起枝头的喜鹊。半夜的凉风吹来了远处的蝉鸣声。稻谷的香气中，人们谈论着来年的丰收景象，耳畔是一阵阵青蛙的应和声。

浓黑的天空中，星光闪烁，远处的山头下起几滴小雨。正想找个地方躲雨，跑过溪边的小桥，往日一直紧邻土地庙的乡村客店就出现在了眼前。

画堂春 · 外湖莲子长参差
张先

外湖莲子长参差，霁山青处鸥飞。水天溶漾画桡迟，人影鉴中移。

桃叶浅声双唱，杏红深色轻衣。小荷障面避斜晖，分得翠阴归。

Spring in Painted Hall
Zhang Xian

The lotus blooms in outer lake grow high and low;
After the rain over green hills fly the gulls white.
The painted boats on rippling water slowly go;
Our shadows move on mirror bright.
Two maidens sing the song of peach leaf in voices low,

Clad in light clothes apricot-red.

They come back with green shadow fed.

关键词

high and low: 对译"参差",直译为"高高低低的"。low与隔句的尾词 go 押韵,且全词都做到了隔句押韵,也是译者韵体译诗的典型作品。

on mirror bright: 对译"鉴中",直译为"在明亮的镜子中"。人在船中,船行水上,水面如镜,人影在镜里移动。译诗保留了如镜的水面这一意象。

译文

外湖长满了错落的莲蓬,雨后的青山泛着青色的氤氲,雪白的鸥鸟在碧水蓝天间飞翔。水天一色,湖波荡漾,画船缓缓前行。人影倒映在水面上,宛如在镜中移动。

歌女们低声浅唱,歌声轻婉。她们所穿的杏红色薄衫,在青山绿水的映衬下,显得更加鲜艳亮丽了。夕阳西下,歌女们采下荷叶遮面,以躲避斜阳。我也似乎在归去的路上分得了一份阴凉。

剪牡丹 · 舟中闻双琵琶 · 野绿连空

张先

野绿连空，天青垂水，素色溶漾都净。柳径无人，堕絮飞无影。汀洲日落人归，修巾薄袂，撷香拾翠相竞。如解凌波，泊烟渚春暝。

彩绦朱索新整。宿绣屏、画船风定。金凤响双槽，弹出今古幽思谁省。玉盘大小乱珠迸。酒上妆面，花艳眉相并。重听。尽汉妃一曲，江空月静。

Peonies Cut Down

Zhang Xian

The green plain extends far and wide,

The azure sky hangs over waterside.

The endless river flows with ripples purified.

On willowy lanes there's no man in sight;

The willow falls down without shadow in flight.

People come back,drowned in slanting sunlight.

Girt with long belt and dressed with thin sleeves,

Girls vie in plucking flowers and green leaves.

They know how to tread on the waves, it seems,

On misty rivershore spring dreams.

Newly adorned with tassels red and ribbons green,

They live behind embroidered screen.

The painted boat goes without breeze.

The golden phoenix on the pipa sings with ease.

Who knows if the woe old or new is played?

Big and small pearls run riot on the plate of jade.

Flowers and eyebrows vie in beauty in vain.

Listen again!

When the princess sings of her dream,

It will calm down the moon and the stream.

关键词

purified: 纯净的，对译"净"，与前两句尾词均押韵。原词全句用了"素色（白色的）""净"来形容这河水，译文以一词以概之，却又加了endless（无尽的）一词，将其意境具体化。增删之间，语言美和音乐美尽显。

tread on: 踩。"凌波"即踩水而行，本出曹植《洛神赋》用"凌波微步，罗袜生尘"。遇到典故，译文便加词意译，为译者"三化论"

之"深化"。

calm down：冷静、宁静。对译"江空月静"，译文未直译江"空"，以静译空，意境既出，也更简洁，保留全词音美的特点。

译文

绿色的原野延伸到天边，青色的天空落到水里，白茫茫的水面上波光浮动，一切都显得干干净净的。栽满柳树的小路上空无一人，柳絮都随风飘远。落日停留在江洲之上，春日装束的妇女们在归家的路上，竞相采芳草、拾翠羽。春季傍晚，有人步履轻盈登上客船，江面上水汽蒸腾，如烟似雾。

女子们整理着身上的彩带，相聚于船舱彩绘的画屏内。风停夜静时，忽然传出两位琵琶女奏响的乐曲，这忧思古往今来又有谁懂？琵琶声犹如大珠小珠落玉盘。酒劲染红了面颊，让琵琶女脸上的妆更艳丽了，她们美艳的双眉紧紧聚拢。再听一曲《昭君怨》，只见江面空阔，静月高挂。

行香子 · 过七里濑 · 一叶舟轻
苏轼

一叶舟轻，双桨鸿惊。水天清、影湛波平。鱼翻藻鉴，鹭点烟汀。过沙溪急，霜溪冷，月溪明。

重重似画，曲曲如屏。算当年、虚老严陵。君臣一梦，今古空名。但远山长，云山乱，晓山青。

Joy of Eternal Union

Passing the Seven-league Shallows

Su Shi

A leaflike boat goes light; At dripping oars wild geese take fright.

Under a sky serene clear shadows float on calm waves green.

Among the mirrored water grass fish play

And egrets dot the riverbank mist-grey.

Thus I go past the sandy brook flowing fast,

The frosted brook cold, The moonlit brook bright to behold.

Hill upon hill is a picturesque scene;

Bend after bend looks like a screen.

I recall those far-away years：

The hermit wasted his life till he grew old;

The emperor shared the same dream with his peers.

Then as now, their fame was left out in the cold.

Only the distant hills outspread till they're unseen,

The cloud-crowned hills look disheveled and dawnlit hills so

green.

关键词

the sandy brook：对译"沙溪"，此处为直译，为浅化译法。
沙溪，实际是指白天之溪，清澈而见沙底，与后文的 frosted brook
（霜溪，清晓之溪）、moonlit brook（月溪，月下之溪）译法同，
写出了三个不同时辰的舟行之景。

those far-away years：对译"当年"，far-away 意为遥远的。
译者不用 past 等词，而以 far-away 点出东汉初年的严子陵隐居垂钓
的典故，今古对照，表达出词人浮生若梦的感慨。years 还与后文
的 peers 隔行押韵。

译文

　　乘着一叶轻舟，双桨带起的水波惊起了岸边的鸿雁。水色清明，水波渐平，人影恢复了平静时的模样。鱼在镜子一样的水面翻跳，白鹭在江中小洲的烟雾中穿行。白天时，溪水清澈见底；清晓时，溪水清冷带霜意；月下时，溪水清亮晶莹。

　　远处的重峦叠嶂，纵看像水墨画，横看如屏风。笑严光当年在此隐居终老，也不曾真正领略到山水佳处。君臣一场，仿佛只是梦醒后的空名。只留下延绵远山，山间乱云，云里青峰。

采桑子 · 轻舟短棹西湖好
欧阳修

轻舟短棹西湖好，绿水逶迤，芳草长堤，隐隐笙歌处处随。
无风水面琉璃滑，不觉船移，微动涟漪，惊起沙禽掠岸飞。

Gathering Mulberry Leaves
Ouyang Xiu

Viewed from a light boat with short oars, West Lake is fair.
Green water winds along
The banks overgrown with sweet grass; here and there
Faintly we hear a flute song.

The water surface is smooth like glass when no wind blows;
I feel the boat moves no more.

Leaving ripples behind, it goes,

The startled waterbirds skim the flat sandy shore.

关键词

viewed from：从这个角度看。译者用被动句式点出了感叹"轻舟短棹西湖好"的主角，从他的视角去看西湖，读者读来身临其境。

leaving ripples behind：对译"微动涟漪"，该句直译为"船前行，将涟漪留在了身后"，拟人化的译文，读来颇生动。

译文

乘着小舟滑动小桨，在蜿蜒碧绿的西湖游赏。长堤上长满了青草，总有隐约的笙歌声围绕在耳边。

无风的湖面像琉璃一样光滑，让人感觉不到船的移动。微微的细浪荡到岸边，惊起了沙滩上的水鸟。

采桑子 · 画船载酒西湖好
欧阳修

画船载酒西湖好，急管繁弦，玉盏催传，稳泛平波任醉眠。
行云却在行舟下，空水澄鲜，俯仰留连，疑是湖中别有天。

Gathering Mulberry Leaves
Ouyang Xiu

West Lake is fine for us in painted boat loaded with wine.

From pipes and strings comes music fast;

From hand to hand jade cups soon passed,

Secure on calming waves, drunk we lie.

Fleeting clouds seem to float beneath our moving boat.

The sky seems near to the dinersnow.

Looking up and below, we will not go away.

It seems there's in the lake another sky.

关键词

comes music fast：音乐来得很快，该句对译"急管繁弦"。译者以一个 come fast 来译"急""繁"二字，好似音乐是有生命的，从管弦里奔涌而出。此为合译之法，是浅化的一种。

fleeting clouds：对译"行云"，直译为"飞逝的云"，行舟下有行云，显然是湖中云的倒影，以此来凸显湖水的清澈。

译文

乘着画船载着美酒在西湖游赏，紧凑的音乐中，人们推杯换盏。稳稳的行船让喝醉的客人安心入眠。

白云好像在船下浮动，天空和湖水清澈明净。仰视蓝天俯视湖面，让我怀疑湖水下面别有一番天地。

采桑子·群芳过后西湖好
欧阳修

群芳过后西湖好，狼籍残红，飞絮濛濛。垂柳阑干尽日风。
笙歌散尽游人去，始觉春空，垂下帘栊，双燕归来细雨中。

Gathering Mulberry Leaves
Ouyang Xiu

All flowers have passed away, West Lake is quiet;
The fallen blooms run riot.
Catkins from willow trees
Beyond the railings fly all day, fluffy in breeze.

Flute songs no longer sung and sightseers gone,
I begin to feel spring alone.

Lowering the blinds in vain,

I see a pair of swallows come back in the rain.

关键词

fluffy：毛茸茸的、松软的，译者以形容词作名词，做了词性转换的等化，代指前文提到的垂柳飞絮，避免了重复用 willow trees（垂柳）一词，简洁明了。

alone：独自的，孤独的。译文以"spring alone（孤独的春天）"对译"春空"，准确表达了词人面对这暮春的一片空寂时惜春恋春的心境。

译文

百花凋零之后的西湖风景依然很美，落花一片，柳絮迷蒙。垂柳在风中随风摇曳。

笙歌声渐渐散去，游人尽兴而归，才开始觉得春的寥落。回到房间放下帘栊，一对燕子在蒙蒙细雨中归来。

浣溪沙 · 堤上游人逐画船
欧阳修

堤上游人逐画船，拍堤春水四垂天。绿杨楼外出秋千。
白发戴花君莫笑，六幺催拍盏频传。人生何处似尊前！

Silk-washing Stream
Ouyang Xiu

With painted boats along the shore sightseers vie;
The sky hangs low on four sides washed by waves of spring.
Green willows throw a swing
Out of the bower high.

Do not laugh at the white hair adorned with red flowers!
To the quick beat of the song of Green Waist

Wine cups are passed in haste.

Where can you find a happier life than drinking hours?

关键词

throw: 扔、掷。throw a swing（掷出一个秋千）对译"出秋千"。原词中的"出"字是画龙点睛之笔，同时突出了秋千和荡秋千的人，使人们仿佛看到了秋千上娇美的身影，听到了欢声笑语。译文以一个 throw 便道出了这种喧闹之境，平添一分盎然。

green Waist: 绿腰，曲调名，是唐代有名的曲子，此处对译"六幺"。译者将其深化，直接点出了其深层含义。

drinking hours: 喝酒的时光，对译"尊前"。该句以反问句译陈述句，加强了"没有什么比喝酒更开心"的肯定语气。

译文

堤上的游人跟随画船行走，湖边的春水拍打着堤岸，水花泛起，水天一色。绿杨后的小楼外，荡起的秋千一次次闪过。

莫要笑话满头白发的老人还头戴鲜花，在《六幺》曲急促的节拍中觥筹交错。人生什么时候还能像现在这样轻松随意呢？

临江仙·离果州作·鸠雨催成新绿
陆游

鸠雨催成新绿，燕泥收尽残红。春光还与美人同。论心空眷眷，分袂却匆匆。

只道真情易写，那知怨句难工。水流云散各西东。半廊花院月，一帽柳桥风。

Riverside Daffodils

Leaving Guozhou

Lu You

The drizzling rain hastens grass to green the place;

Swallows peck clods blended with fallen red,

Spring is as beautiful as a rosy face;

With a lingering heart

She's unwilling to part.

I thought true feeling easy to paint;
But know not it's hard to voice a complaint.
Water flows east or west and clouds wide spread,
Flowers in the yard steeped in moonlight,
On willowy bridge my hat is filled with breeze light.

关键词

the drizzling rain: 毛毛雨，对译"鸠雨"，相传鹁鸠鸟每逢阴天就会将配偶赶走，等到天晴就又将其呼唤回来。因此民间有俗语道："天将雨，鸠逐妇。"译者将其浅化，却以 drizzling 一词抓住了春雨蒙蒙的特征。

a rosy face: 对译"美人"，此处为意译，译者以"红扑扑的脸"代指年轻的美人，形象生动，且 face 与上文的 place 也押韵，以达音美。

light: 轻轻的。该句对译"一帽柳桥风"，译者加 light 一词修饰 breeze，直译为"我的帽子灌满了轻轻的微风"，意美传达得很准确，且也凑了韵，和 moonlight 押尾韵。

译文

鹁鸠鸟的叫声中，春雨将万物染成了绿色，燕子将凋落的花瓣和着泥土做成鸟巢。这春光和美人一样，在一起时恋恋不舍，分别时又总是匆匆。

　　只知道真情易说，哪知道却难以描述真切。我们即将像水流和云一样各奔东西。月亮照亮了回廊花院，旅途中的和风吹动帽檐。

临江仙·千里潇湘接蓝浦
秦观

千里潇湘接蓝浦，兰桡昔日曾经。月高风定露华清。微波澄不动，冷浸一天星。

独倚危樯情悄悄，遥闻妃瑟泠泠。新声含尽古今情。曲终人不见，江上数峰青。

Riverside Daffodils
Qin Guan

I roam along the thousand-mile blue river-shore,

Where floated Poet Qu's orchid boat of yore.

The moon is high, the wind goes down, the dew is clear.

Ripples tranquil appear,

A skyful of stars shiver.

Silent, leaning against the high mast on the river,

I seem to hear the lute of the fairy queen.

Her music moves all hearts now as before.

When her song ends, she is not seen,

Leaving, on the stream but peaks green.

关键词

of yore：很久以前，昔日，对译"昔日曾经"。该句延续了原词的倒装手法，做到了形似，并点明了"兰桡"代指的 Poet Qu（屈原），词人和屈原、今日和昔日得以相连，原词的深层之义得以传递。

moves all hearts：与后文的 now as before（现在和以前一样）一起），对译"含尽古今情"。此处为意译，直译为"感动所有的心灵"，以 all 表达"尽"之意。

译文

千里潇湘清澈碧绿，屈原的兰舟曾经经过此地。明月高挂，清风徐徐，玉露清莹。江面上波澜不惊，星月的寒光反射在水面上。

独自斜靠在高高的桅杆上，心中无限忧思，远远传来清冷的瑟声，低低诉说着千古幽情。一曲奏完，云音消散，只剩江两边数不尽的青峰孤耸。

念奴娇·过洞庭·洞庭青草

张孝祥

洞庭青草，近中秋，更无一点风色。玉界琼田三万顷，着我扁舟一叶。素月分辉，明河共影，表里俱澄澈。悠然心会，妙处难与君说。

应念岭海经年，孤光自照，肝胆皆冰雪。短发萧骚襟袖冷，稳泛沧溟空阔。尽挹西江，细斟北斗，万象为宾客。扣舷独啸，不知今夕何夕。

The Charm of a Maiden Singer

Pass the Lake Dongting

Zhang Xiaoxiang

Lake Dongting,Lake Green Grass,

Near the Mid-autumn night,Unruffled for no winds pass,

Like thirty thousand acres of jade bright

Dotted with the leaflike boat of mine.

The skies with pure moonbeams o'erflow;

The water surface paved with moonshine:

Brightness above,brightness below.

My heart with the moon becomes one,Felicity to share with none.

Thinking of the southwest,where I passed a year,

To lonely pure moonlight skin,I feel my heart and soul snow-and-ice-clear.

Although my hair is short and sparse,my gown too thin,

In the immense expanse I keep floating up.

Drinking wine from the River West

And using Dipper as wine cup,I invite Nature to be my guest.

Beating time aboard and crooning alone.

I sink deep into time and place unknown.

关键词

dotted with：点缀其间的。三万顷的湖水，载一叶扁舟，一个 "点缀" 译得意境准确可观。

paved with：铺就。此句对译 "明河共影"，直译为 "月光铺就的 水面"。且同是 "月光"，上下文分别以 moonbeams、moonshine、 moonlight 译之，足见匠心。

immense expanse：无边无际的广阔区域，对译 "沧溟空阔"。 词人泛舟于横无际涯的洞庭湖上， "任凭风浪起，稳坐钓鱼台" 的襟怀得以体现。

sink deep into：深陷入。此句对译"不知今夕何夕"，词人已忘情于月白无风之夜，忘情于与大自然的交融之中，怎会记得今夕是何年？若直译，则为"我陷入了未知的时空"。

译文

洞庭湖边草木丛生，在中秋将至时，没有一丝风吹过的痕迹。三万顷洁白清亮如明镜般的湖水，载着我的一叶扁舟。皎洁的明月与灿烂的银河投下倒影，水天共色，一片清净澄澈。这种美景的妙处只能心领神会，却难以向诸位描述分享。

回想在岭南的那些年，明月也只能顾影自怜，但它的胸怀依然如冰雪般清透。如今我须发变得稀少，冷风吹动衣襟袖口，却安然泛舟于烟波浩渺的湖面上。待我舀尽西江的水，仔细斟满北斗星做的酒盏，邀请世间万象做我的宾客。我拍打着船舷独自高歌，不知道此时是何年。

张孝祥

张孝祥，字安国，别号于湖居士，历阳乌江（今安徽和县乌江镇）人，唐代著名诗人张籍七世孙。状元及第，善诗文，尤工词，风格宏伟豪放，为"豪放派"代表词人，有《于湖居士文集》《于湖词》等传世。

水调歌头·金山观月·江山自雄丽
张孝祥

江山自雄丽，风露与高寒。寄声月姊，借我玉鉴此中看。幽壑鱼龙悲啸，倒影星辰摇动，海气夜漫漫。涌起白银阙，危驻紫金山。

表独立，飞霞佩，切云冠。漱冰濯雪，眇视万里一毫端。回首三山何处，闻道群仙笑我，要我欲俱还。挥手从此去，翳凤更骖鸾。

Prelude to Water Melody
The Moon Viewed on Golden Hill
Zhang Xiaoxiang

The lofty mountain stands in view,
When wind is high and cold is dew.

I'd ask the Goddess of the Moon,

To lend me her jade mirror soon

To see in deep water fish and dragon sigh

And stars shiver as if fallen from on high.

The boundless sea mingles her breath with boundless night.

On the waves surges the palace silver-white;

The Golden Hill Temple frowns on the height.

Alone it towers high, Girt with a rainbow bright,

Its crown would scrape the sky. With ice and snow purified,

It overlooks the boundless land far and wide.

Looking back; where are the fairy hills two or three?

The immortals may laugh at me; They ask me to go with them to

the sea.

Waving my hand, I'll leave the land, with a phoenix as my

canopy.

关键词

mingle：使混合。此句对译"海气夜漫漫"，直译为"无边无际的海将它的呼吸和无边无际的黑夜融合在一起"，意美尽显。

towers high：高耸。此句对译"表独立"，卓然而立。译者将 alone 前置，强调了词人遗世独立的姿态。

canopy：华盖。此句对译"翳凤更骖鸾"——那鸾鸟驾驶，以凤羽为车盖的马车，译者在此以局部译整体，用凤羽华盖代指马车。

译文

　　江山雄伟壮丽，夜晚登临，看到露珠点点，微风吹拂，不禁感到山间些许寒意。托人传话给月亮，是否可以借我明镜来欣赏这绝妙景色。幽深的山谷中鱼龙发出悲凄的长啸，倒映在水中的星辰随水波晃动，黑夜漫长，海面上水汽弥漫，金山寺仿佛白银砌成，从海浪中升腾而起，驻在了紫金山顶。

　　我站在山巅，戴着飞霞做成的玉佩，束着高耸的头冠，一派遗世独立的模样，沐浴在冰雪般的月光中，整个世界通透洁净，万里外的细微之处也能看得清楚。回首遥望仙界的三座仙山，听闻神仙们笑我，邀我与他们同游，乘上鸾鸟驾驶的华美车子，挥挥手扬长而去。

水调歌头 · 游览 · 瑶草一何碧
黄庭坚

瑶草一何碧，春入武陵溪。溪上桃花无数，花上有黄鹂。我欲穿花寻路，直入白云深处，浩气展虹霓。只恐花深里，红露湿人衣。

坐玉石，倚玉枕。拂金徽。谪仙何处？无人伴我白螺杯。我为灵芝仙草，不为朱唇丹脸，长啸亦何为？醉舞下山去，明月逐人归。

Prelude to Water Melody

Sightseeing

Huang Tingjian

How could grass be so green? O Spring

Enters the fairy stream. Where countless peach blooms beam,

And on the branch of the tree golden orioles sing.

I try to find a way through the flowers so gay,

Straight into clouds so white, To breathe a rainbow bright,

But I'm afraid in the depth of the flowers in my view,

My sleeves would be wet with rosy dew.

I sit on a stone and, Lean on a pillow of jade,

A tune on golden lute is played. Where is the poet of the fairyland?

Who would drink up with me my spiral cup?

I come to seek for the immortal's trace,

Not for the rouged lips and powdered face.

Why should I long, long croon?

Drunk,I would dance downhill soon, Followed by the bright moon.

关键词

fairy stream: 仙流，对译"武陵溪"，此处的武陵溪代指桃花源，故译者将其浅化，以仙流译之。

breathe: 呼出，透气，以动词译名词，对译"浩气"。该句词人化用了《桃花源记》的典故，"一直走向白云深处的山顶，彩虹之巅展现浩气"，译者加了 bright（明亮的、有希望的）一词来修饰彩虹，不仅凑了韵，同时也烘托了词人以理想世界表达对现实不满的心境。

rosy dew：玫瑰色的、粉红色的露水，对译"红露"。此处是从王维的诗句"山路元无雨，空翠湿人衣"（《山中》）脱化而来，词人把"空翠"换成"红露"，"红露"即"花露"，故译者以rosy译之，很是贴切。

译文

瑶草多么碧绿，春天已经来到武陵溪。花瓣铺满水面，引来了黄鹂鸟。我想要穿过花丛寻找出路，却走到了白云深处，彩虹浩瀚地展现在我眼前。只怕花丛深处，香露打湿了我的衣服。

坐在玉石上，倚着玉枕，抚摩金徽。被贬下凡尘的仙人在哪？没人陪我用螺杯喝酒。我为寻灵芝仙草，也不是为了容颜姣好，这究竟是为了什么？喝醉了就手舞足蹈地走下山吧，明月仿佛也在催我回家。

离亭燕·一带江山如画
张昇

一带江山如画，风物向秋潇洒。水浸碧天何处断？霁色冷光相射。蓼屿荻花洲，掩映竹篱茅舍。

天际客帆高挂，烟外酒旗低迓。多少六朝兴废事，尽入渔樵闲话。怅望倚危栏，红日无言西下。

Swallows Leaving Pavilion
Zhang Bian

So picturesque the land by riverside,
In autumn tints the scenery is purified.
Without a break green waves merge into azure sky,
The sunbeams after rain take chilly dye.
Bamboo fence dimly seen amid the reeds

And thatch-roofed cottages overgrown with weeds.

Among white clouds are lost white sails,
And where smoke coils up slow,
There wineshop streamers hang low.
How many of the fisherman's and woodman's tales
Are told about the Six Dynasties' fall and rise!
Saddened,I lean upon the tower's rails,
Mutely the sun turns cold and sinks in western skies.

关键词

so picturesque：如此风景如画的。译者用了倒装句式，并加了程度副词 so，强调了江山如画，也让 riverside 与下文的 purified 得以押韵。

merge into：并入、融入。"浸"，指水天融为一体。

azure：蔚蓝色的。

thatch-roofed：茅草屋顶。

coils up：卷起来。smoke coils up slow，对译"烟外"，烟雾笼罩的岸边，此句直译为"烟雾缭绕缓慢升起"，契合全词所述的雨后初晴之景。

saddened：难过、黯然。怅望，即怀着怅惘的心情远望。译者以 saddened 译之，引出下文太阳西下的苍凉之感。

译文

金陵的风光美丽如画，秋季的景色更具风韵。晴空高远如水浸洗过，一望无际，雨后的天色与秋水相辉映，泛着清冷的光芒。湖心的小岛上蓼草荻花丛生，掩映着竹篱茅舍。

远处客船的帆高悬，酒肆外的酒旗低垂，那些六朝的兴衰往事，如今已成为渔民樵夫的闲时谈资。站在高楼上惆怅地倚着栏杆，看斜阳默默落下西山。

张　昇

　　张昇，字杲卿，同州夏阳（今陕西韩城）人，官至御史中丞、参知政事兼枢密使，以太子太师致仕。词作仅存两首，其中《离亭燕》咏景怀古，苍凉不失浪漫，被《三国演义》作为开篇词使用的明人杨慎名作《临江仙·滚滚长江东逝水》，便是从此篇中受到启发创作而成。

辑四

得闲

忘机

行香子·树绕村庄
秦观

　　树绕村庄，水满陂塘；倚东风、豪兴徜徉；小园几许，收尽春光。有桃花红，李花白，菜花黄。

　　远远围墙，隐隐茅堂；飏青旗、流水桥旁。偶然乘兴，步过东冈。正莺儿啼，燕儿舞，蝶儿忙。

Song of Pilgrimage
Qin Guan

The village girt with trees, The pools overbrim with water clear.

Leaning on eastern breeze, My spirit soars up higher and freer.

The garden small has inhaled vernal splendor all:

Peach red, plums mellow and rape flowers yellow.

Far off stand mossy walls, Dim, dim the thatched halls,

The wineshop streamers fly; Under the bridge water flows by.

By luck in spirits high I pass where the eastern hills rise.

Orioles sing their song, Swallows dance along, Busy are butterflies.

关键词

soar up: 本是"高飞，翱翔，升高"之意，译者还辅以 higher and freer（更高、更自由）来对译"豪兴徜徉"之"豪"，凸显词人兴致之高。

mossy: 长满青苔的。原词中只说了围墙，未提青苔。此为译意，加了青苔这一具体意象，和后面的茅堂相对，更切合原词的意境。

译文

绿树围绕着村庄，春水溢满池塘，我沐浴着东风，乘兴安闲自在地徘徊在小院，将春光尽收眼底。满眼都是红色的桃花、白色的李花、金灿灿的菜花。

远远的一排围墙里，隐约有几间茅草屋。青色的旗子随风飘扬，我跟着流水来到桥旁。乘着偶然的兴致，走过东面的山岗。那里莺儿鸣啼，燕儿飞舞，蝶儿匆忙。

鹧鸪天·游鹅湖醉书酒家壁·
春入平原荠菜花

辛弃疾

春入平原荠菜花，新耕雨后落群鸦。多情白发春无奈，晚日青帘酒易赊。

闲意态，细生涯。牛栏西畔有桑麻。青裙缟袂谁家女？去趁蚕生看外家。

Partridges in the Sky
Written on the Wall of a Wine Shop
Xin Qiji

Spring comes to the plain with shepherd's purse in flower,
A flock of crows fly down on new-tilled fields after shower.

What could an old man with young heart do on days fine?

At dusk he drinks on credit in the shop of wine.

People with ease do what they please.

West of the cattle pen there're hemps and mulberries.

Why should the newly-wed in black skirt and white coat run

To see her parents before cocoons are spun?

关键词

an old man with young heart: 对译"多情白发",此处为意译。以"年轻的心"对译"多情"。

ease: 容易,舒适。两句合为一句,直译为"人们舒适地做着他们喜欢的事",岂不是"闲意态,细生涯"?

译文

春天降临,茂盛的荠菜花开满了整个平原。广袤的土地刚刚经过开垦,春雨灌溉后,引来群鸦觅食。诸多情愁催生白发,盎然的春天也无济于事,只有晚上去小酒馆借酒消愁。

人们的神态悠闲自在,日子也过得细致。牛栏西边种满了桑和麻。不知谁家的农妇,趁着新蚕孵出之前,赶着去娘家看看。

鹧鸪天 · 代人赋 · 陌上柔桑破嫩芽
辛弃疾

陌上柔桑破嫩芽，东邻蚕种已生些。平冈细草鸣黄犊，斜日寒林点暮鸦。

山远近，路横斜，青旗沽酒有人家。城中桃李愁风雨，春在溪头荠菜花。

Partridges in the Sky
Xin Qiji

The tender twigs begin to spout along the lane;
The silkworm's eggs of my east neighbor have come out.
The yellow calves grazing fine grass bawl on the plain;
At sunset in the cold forest crows fly about.
The mountains extend far and near;

Lanes crisscross there and here.

Blue streamers fly where wine shops appear.

Peach and plum blossoms in the town fear wind and showers,

But spring dwells by the creekside where blossom wildflowers.

关键词

fly about：飞来飞去。太阳西斜，暮鸦晚归，仿佛一团团墨点。补足暮鸦的动作，将其具象化，比名词直译更有画面感。

there and here：到处，补足 lanes crisscross（交错的路）的状语，对译"路横斜"，也和 far and near 构成对仗押韵，准确地保留了原文的结构。

dwell：居住，栖身。"春在溪头"，以"栖身"译"在"，原文的意境表达得更为生动准确。

译文

田边柔弱的桑树枝上露出青青的嫩芽，东边邻居家的蚕种已经孵出小蚕。小黄牛在平坦的山坡上一边吃着细草一边叫唤。夕阳里，乌鸦在干秃的树枝上停留，为这春寒更添了一些寒意。

远远近近的青山，纵横交错的小路，远处的酒幌子告知人们这里还有卖酒的人家。城里的桃花虽美，却害怕风雨吹打，只有溪边野蛮生长的荠菜花才代表了春天真正来临。

清平乐·村居·茅檐低小
辛弃疾

茅檐低小，溪上青青草。醉里吴音相媚好，白发谁家翁媪？
大儿锄豆溪东，中儿正织鸡笼。最喜小儿亡赖，溪头卧剥莲蓬。

Pure Serene Music

Xin Qiji

The thatched roof slants low,

Beside the brook green grasses grow.

Who talks with drunken Southern voice to please?

White-haired man and wife at their ease.

East of the brook their eldest son is hoeing weeds;

Their second son now makes a cage for hens he feeds.

How pleasant to see their spoiled youngest son who heeds

Nothing but lies by brookside and pods lotus seeds!

关键词

at their ease：放松的，不拘束的。此处为意译，以一问一答的设问句直接点明白发翁媪的心情。

heeds：留心、注意。最留心的当属小儿子，heed 加强了 pleasant 的程度，突出了"最喜"。又和上下文的 weeds、feeds、seeds 押韵。

译文

草屋的房檐又低又小，溪边长满了青青的细草。酒醉时，耳边的吴音都显得温柔美好，那满头白发的老妇人是谁家的？

大儿子在溪水东边的豆田里锄草，二儿子正在编织鸡笼。最惹人喜爱的小儿子，正淘气地躺在溪边，剥着刚刚摘下的莲蓬。

昭君怨·咏荷上雨·午梦扁舟花底
杨万里

午梦扁舟花底，香满西湖烟水。急雨打篷声，梦初惊。
却是池荷跳雨，散了真珠还聚。聚作水银窝，泻清波。

Lament of a Fair Lady
Raindrops on Lotus Leaves
Yang Wanli

1 nap at noon in a leaflike boat beneath lotus flowers;
Their fragrance spreads over mist-veiled West Lake.
I hear my boat's roof beaten by sudden showers,
And startled,I awake.

I find on lotus leaves leap drops of rain;

Like pearls they scatter and get together again.

They melt then into liquid silver

Flowing down the rippling river.

关键词

leaflike boat：像叶子一样的船，对译"扁舟"，摹状，比一般译作"small boat"更见神韵。

on lotus leaves：在荷叶上，对译"池荷"跳雨，既是跳雨，便将其意象具体化，点出荷叶，和后文雨点在荷叶上聚散的形态做呼应，此为加词深化之法。

译文

午睡时梦见乘舟在花间穿行，湖面上的水汽里飘出醉人的香气。雨落船篷之声，将我从梦中惊醒。

雨滴在池塘中的荷叶上跳动，一滴滴雨像散落的珍珠在荷叶中心聚集，仿佛水银般晶莹。雨水压弯了荷叶，清澈的水流顺着荷叶流入池塘。

杨万里

　　杨万里，字廷秀，号诚斋，吉州吉水（今江西吉水）人。一生作诗两万多首，传世作品达四千二百首，并创造了语言浅近明白、清新自然，富有幽默情趣的"诚斋体"，被誉为一代诗宗，与陆游、尤袤、范成大并称"中兴四大诗人"。著有《诚斋集》。

浣溪沙 · 麻叶层层苘叶光
苏轼

麻叶层层苘叶光，谁家煮茧一村香？隔篱娇语络丝娘。
垂白杖藜抬醉眼，捋青捣𪌭软饥肠。问言豆叶几时黄？

Silk-washing Stream
Su Shi

The leaves of jute and hemp are thick and lush in this land;
The scent of boiling cocoons in the village spreads.
Across the fence young maidens prate while reeling threads.

An old man raises dim-sighted eyes, cane in hand;
He blends new wheat with old and says, "Eat if you please."
I ask him when will yellow the leaves of green peas.

关键词

thick and lush：茂盛的、茂密的、郁郁葱葱的。thick，lush 均有茂密意，此处二词叠用，对译"层层"，为意译。

blend：混合，调制。对译"抒青捣㸑"，此处为意译，老农将尚未成熟的新麦做成干粮果腹，译者结合了原词的写作背景，透过老农的行为叙写了春旱灾难之重。

译文

眼前的层层麻叶散发着光泽，不知谁家煮豆，香气传遍了整个村子。篱笆那边传来缫丝女子悦耳的谈笑声。

拄着手杖的白发老人双眼无神，㧟下未成熟的麦粒准备做成干粮果腹。我忍不住上前关切地问道：豆类作物几时才能成熟呢？

鹧鸪天 · 林断山明竹隐墙
苏轼

林断山明竹隐墙。乱蝉衰草小池塘。翻空白鸟时时见，照水红蕖细细香。

村舍外，古城旁，杖藜徐步转斜阳。殷勤昨夜三更雨，又得浮生一日凉。

Partridges in the Sky
Su Shi

Through forest breaks appear hills and bamboo-screened wall;
Cicadas shrill o' er withered grass near a pool small.
White birds are seen now and then looping in the air;
Pink lotus blooms on lakeside exude fragrance spare.
Beyond the cots, Near ancient town,

Cane in hand,I stroll round while the sun's slanting down.

Thanks to the welcome rain which fell when night was deep,

Now in my floating life one more fresh day I reap.

关键词

a pool small：小池塘。译者将修饰词 small 后置，与上句句尾的 wall 押韵。

spare：此处取"少量的"之意。exude fragrance spare，散发出少量的香气，对译"细细香"，spare 也与上句的 air 押韵。

thanks to the welcome rain：对译"殷勤（多承，有劳）"，三更时下雨了，译者连用了 thanks to 和 welcome 来形容词人的感激与喜悦之情，结合词人当时被贬谪的境遇来看，此处堪称"词眼"，隐藏着他的无限感慨。

译文

蓊蓊郁郁的树林尽头，高耸的山峰显现出来，眼前茂密的竹林将高高的院墙围得严严实实的。蝉声密集，小池塘里满是衰草。天空中有白色的鸟儿飞过，荷花倒映在水中，散发阵阵清香。

村庄外面，古城墙下。我拄着拐杖漫步在斜阳里。还好昨晚下了一场细雨，让人又偷得一日清凉。

浣溪沙·游蕲水清泉寺·山下兰芽短浸溪
苏轼

游蕲水清泉寺，寺临兰溪，溪水西流。

山下兰芽短浸溪，松间沙路净无泥，潇潇暮雨子规啼。

谁道人生无再少？门前流水尚能西！休将白发唱黄鸡。

Silk-washing Stream

Su Shi

In the stream below the hill there drowns the orchid bud;

On sandy path between pine trees you see no mud.

Shower by shower falls the rain while cuckoos sing.

Who says an old man can't return unto his spring?

Before Clear Fountain's Temple water still flows west.

Why can't the cock still crow though with a snow-white crest?

关键词

return unto：回到。全句为意译，对译"谁道人生无再少"，直译为"谁说老人就不能回到他的春天"，以"春天"译"年少"，意美尽现。

crow：欢叫。译者以反问句对译陈述句，加强其肯定语气，"难道鸡冠已白的鸡就不能欢叫吗"。"白发""黄鸡"本就比喻世事匆促，光景催年，译者在此保留该意象，以鸡喻人，表达词人不服衰老的宣言和对生活的热爱。

译文

山脚下兰草的新芽浸润在溪水里，松林间的沙路，洁净无泥。傍晚细雨潇潇，传来几声杜鹃的叫声。

谁说人生不能回到年少时期？门前的流水都还能向西边流去。不要在老年才感叹时光的飞逝啊！

定风波·莫听穿林打叶声
苏轼

三月七日，沙湖道中遇雨。雨具先去，同行皆狼狈，余独不觉。已而遂晴，故作此词。

莫听穿林打叶声，何妨吟啸且徐行。竹杖芒鞋轻胜马，谁怕？一蓑烟雨任平生。

料峭春风吹酒醒，微冷，山头斜照却相迎。回首向来萧瑟处，归去，也无风雨也无晴。

Calming the Waves
Su Shi

Listen not to the rain beating against the trees.

Why don't you slowly walk and chant at ease?

Better than saddled horse I like sandals and cane.

O I would fain, Spend a straw-cloaked life in mist and rain.

Drunken, I'm sobered by vernal wind shrill, And rather chill.

In front I see the slanting sun atop the hill;

Turning my head, I see the dreary beaten track.

Let me go back!

Impervious to wind, rain or shine, I'll have my will.

关键词

at ease：自由自在。此处为典型的加词凑韵，ease 和 trees 押韵。一个"自由自在"把词人在雨中悠然徐行的旷达心态展露无遗。

fain：欣然、乐意。此句对译"谁怕？"，译者直接点明词人的态度，不仅不怕，还乐意之至！

impervious：不受影响的，无动于衷的。此句对译"也无风雨也无晴"，无论风云变幻，起起落落，我自由我（I'll have my will）。结合苏东坡的经历来看，他虽处逆境，屡遭贬谪而始终从容、达观的生活态度极为动人。

译文

不要在意雨滴穿过树林敲打树叶的声音，不要忌讳吟咏长啸着从容前行。拄着竹杖穿着芒鞋，比骑马还要轻松。有什么可怕的。穿着蓑衣在风雨里过一辈子也能处之泰然。

微凉的春风吹醒我的醉意，有点凉，山头的斜阳却赶忙来迎接我。回头看刚才走过的一路风雨，回家。管他风雨还是晴。

蝶恋花·春涨一篙添水面
范成大

春涨一篙添水面。芳草鹅儿，绿满微风岸。画舫夷犹湾百转，横塘塔近依前远。

江国多寒农事晚。村北村南，谷雨才耕遍。秀麦连冈桑叶贱，看看尝面收新茧。

Butterflies in Love with Flowers
Fan Chengda

In spring the water rises high,

The grassy shore is greened by the light breeze.

Where swim the geese,

The painted boats move slowly on the winding streams,

The tower is still far away, though near it seems.

The weather's cold by riverside,

The fields are not tilled far and wide

Till the season of rain comes nigh.

Wheat and mulberry leaves spread a green hue,

Soon we may taste the grain and reap the cocoon new.

关键词

is greened by: 被染绿。此句对译"绿满微风岸"，直译为"那长满草的河岸被微风染绿"，意境全出，诗意盎然。

spread a green hue: 涂上了绿色，hue 为"色调"意。此句对译"秀麦连冈桑叶贱"，译者未直译，而以"麦子和桑叶都涂上了绿色"，点明了时令——春麦已结秀穗，随风起伏，连冈成片，山冈上桑树茂盛，故而桑叶卖得很贱。

译文

春日，融化的冬雪让水面涨了一篙深。青草白鹅，微风将岸边染成了绿色。彩船在九曲的小河里慢慢前行，横塘前的塔近在眼前，却又难以抵达。

江南水乡多春寒，农事也无法开展。村南村北，谷雨时节才能开耕。春麦上的秀穗铺满山冈，桑树上长满了桑叶。很快就能尝到新面，收获新蚕茧。

范成大

范成大，字至能，一字幼元，晚号石湖居士，吴县（今江苏苏州）人。与杨万里、陆游、尤袤合称"中兴四大诗人"，其作品在南宋末年即产生广泛影响，到清初更有"家剑南而户石湖"的说法。其词多婉丽清新，亦有清旷豪宕之作。著有《石湖集》等。

渔家傲·平岸小桥千嶂抱
王安石

平岸小桥千嶂抱。柔蓝一水萦花草。茅屋数间窗窈窕。尘不到。时时自有春风扫。

午枕觉来闻语鸟。欹眠似听朝鸡早。忽忆故人今总老。贪梦好。茫然忘了邯郸道。

Pride of Fishermen

Wang Anshi

Surrounded by peaks, a bridge flies from shore to shore;

A soft blue stream flows through flowers before the door.

A few thatched houses with windows I adore.

There comes no dust,

The place is swept by vernal breeze in fitful gusts.

I hear birds twitter when awake from nap at noon;

I wonder in my bed why the cock crows so soon.

Thinking of my friends who have all grown old,

Why indulge in a dream of gold?

Do not forget the way to glory is rough and cold!

关键词

adore: 喜欢。窈窕,幽深的样子。此处为意译,译者以"喜欢的"对译幽深秀美的感觉,以便与上文的 shore, door 押韵。

fitful gusts: 一阵阵的风,此句直译为"这里被一阵阵的和风吹过"。译者用 vernal breeze 和 gusts 一起译这时时春风,以凑韵,达到音律美。

glory: 荣耀。此句直译为"不要忘了通往荣耀的路是坎坷而冰冷的"。邯郸道,比喻求取功名之道路,亦指仕途,故译者以 glory 译之,表达了词人此时贪爱闲适的午梦,已丢却建功树名之梦。

译文

　　层峦叠嶂,环抱着小桥流水,溪水青碧,萦绕着花草。溪畔有数间茅檐屋舍,和煦的春风时时吹拂,使它们窗明几净,不染尘埃。

　　午睡醒来听到鸟儿清脆的啼叫,倚枕而眠似乎听到了当年上早朝时的鸡鸣声,忽然忆起故人旧事,如今也都已经老去。现在的我贪图安逸闲适,早已忘却那漫漫仕途。

王安石

　　王安石，字介甫，号半山，抚州临川（今江西抚州）人，曾主持轰动天下的变法运动。其诗"学杜得其瘦硬"，擅长说理与修辞，晚年诗风含蓄深沉、深婉不迫，以丰神远韵的风格在北宋诗坛自成一家，世称"王荆公体"；其词作不多，风格高峻，瘦削雅素，一洗五代绮靡旧习。有《王临川集》《临川集拾遗》等作存世。

西江月·照野弥弥浅浪
苏轼

顷在黄州,春夜行蕲水中,过酒家饮。酒醉,乘月至一溪桥上,解鞍曲肱,醉卧少休。及觉已晓,乱山攒拥,流水锵然,疑非尘世也。书此语桥柱上。

照野弥弥浅浪,横空隐隐层霄。障泥未解玉骢骄,我欲醉眠芳草。

可惜一溪风月,莫教踏碎琼瑶。解鞍欹枕绿杨桥,杜宇一声春晓。

The moon over the West River
Su Shi

Wavelet on wavelet glimmers by shore;
Cloud on cloud dimly appears in the sky.

Unsaddled is my white-jadelike horse;

Drunk, asleep in the sweet grass I'll lie.

My horse's hoofs may break, I'm afraid,

The breeze-rippled brook paved by moonlit jade.

I tether my horse to a bough of green willow.

Near the bridge where I pillow

My head on arms and sleep till the cuckoo's song awakes

A spring daybreak.

关键词

wavelet on wavelet, cloud on cloud: 对译"弥弥浅浪""隐隐层霄"。译文调整了语序，保留了原词的工整对仗之形美。

a bough of green willow: 系马绿柳枝。此处为译者加词"深化"，这一意象原文是没有的，加词后 willow 和 pillow 押韵，意象也更具体化。

译文

月下小溪，春水跃动翻出浅浪，空中稀云，隐隐约约飘浮不定。马身上的马鞍还来不及卸下，我就想在这芳草中醉卧。

这春溪风月如此可爱，千万不能让马儿踩碎那水中月。解下马鞍当枕头，躺在绿杨桥边进入梦乡。一声杜鹃啼鸣，天已破晓。

摸鱼子 · 高爱山隐居 · 爱吾庐
张炎

爱吾庐、傍湖千顷，苍茫一片清润。晴岚暖翠融融处，花影倒窥天镜。沙浦迥。看野水涵波，隔柳横孤艇。眠鸥未醒。甚占得莼乡，都无人见，斜照起春暝。

还重省。岂料山中秦晋，桃源今度难认。林间即是长生路，一笑原非捷径。深更静。待散发吹箫，跨鹤天风冷。凭高露饮。正碧落尘空，光摇半壁，月在万松顶。

Groping for Fish

Hermitage in Mount High Love

Zhang Yan

I love my cot by the lakeside

So fair and wide,

A vast expanse so vague and clear.

On fine days the far-flung hills warm appear,

With flowers reflected in the mirror of the skies.

The sand beach far away,I seem

To see the rippling water beam,

Under the willow trees a lonely boat lies.

The gulls asleep, not yet awake,

Unseen in my native village by the lake.

The setting sun would bring

Twilight to spring.

I meditate:

Who can anticipate

Even Peach Blossom Land

Will witness dynasties fall or stand?

The pathway in the woods will lead to a long life.

I laugh, for it is not a shortcut to win in strife.

It's calm when deep is night,

I would play on my flute with loosened hair

And ride my crane to brave the cold wind in my flight.

I would drink dew on high

And waft in the air.

The moon atop the pines sheds its light

Over the conquered land far and nigh.

关键词

far-flung：遥远的。此句为意译，直译为"在晴日，遥远的群山也温暖了起来"。

native village：故乡的村庄，对译"莼乡"——此处用了张翰在外做官思念家乡莼羹、鲈鱼脍的典故，译者用了浅化的译法。

strife：争斗。to win in strife 为译者加词，strife 与 life 凑了韵，直译为"这不是在争斗中取胜的捷径"——"隐居"不能成了出仕求官的捷径啊，译者将词人的心境明白译出了。

译文

我爱我生活的家园，草庐依傍着千顷湖泊，烟波苍茫清凉朗澈。天晴时，山间雾气弥漫暖意融融，斑驳的花影倒映在湖水中。远处有沙滩，看湖水荡漾，隔岸柳树下停着一只孤舟。鸥鸟依然在沉睡，这里正是盛产莼菜的地方，人们都没有发现，只有夕阳预示着春日的傍晚来临。

再三思忖也不知道山中停驻的光景是秦朝还是晋朝，如今见到桃花源也是难以辨认。隐居林间便是长生之道，我笑道这并非登仙的捷径。夜深林静，我要散下头发吹起玉箫，在清冷的夜风中跨鹤登仙。在高处以露水为饮，此时夜空澄澈，月影照在半面山壁上，明月高悬在松林之上。

张 炎

张炎，字叔夏，号玉田，临安（今浙江杭州）人。南宋覆灭后曾北游燕赵谋官，后失意南归，长期寓居临安，落魄而终。精通音律，著有《词源》，论词乐词艺。其词多身世之慨，激越苍凉。著有《山中白云词》。

西江月·断送一生惟有
黄庭坚

老夫既戒酒不饮，遇宴集，独醒其旁。坐客欲得小词，援笔为赋。

断送一生惟有，破除万事无过。远山横黛蘸秋波，不饮旁人笑我。

花病等闲瘦弱，春愁无处遮拦。杯行到手莫留残，不道月斜人散。

The Moon over the West River
Written for Wine after Abstinence
Huang Tingjian

Nothing dissipates life as you,
Nor rids it of sorrow new.
Before blue-hill-like brow and wave-like eye,
I should be laughed at if I don't drink my cup dry.

For no reason the flower fades.

Could I bar spring grief which invades?

Leave no cup in hand undrunk!

Don't wait till all are gone and the moon sunk.

关键词

rid of：摆脱，消除。此句为意译，直译为"不能把它（酒）从新的悲伤中去除"，译者点出了词人被贬谪后企图以酒浇愁的心态，既有新伤，怎能无酒？

blue-hill-like brow：对译"远山横黛"，指眉毛。《西京杂记》称："（卓）文君姣好，眉色如望远山。"又，汉赵飞燕妹合德为薄眉，号"远山黛"，见伶玄《赵飞燕外传》。故"远山黛"是极具中华文化色彩的，译者以 blue-hill-like 点出了眉毛的形态，做到了意象的对等，十分贴切。

wave-like eye：对译"秋波"，指眼波，译文也做到了意象对等，和"远山横黛"一起，均描摹了酒席宴上侍酒歌女的情态。

译文

我唯靠着酒度过这一生，但消磨万事也没什么过错。身边的女子暗送秋波劝我饮酒，我不喝她就会笑我。

花像得病了一样瘦弱，更显出春天的忧愁。酒杯拿在手里就请一饮而尽吧，别说什么月缺人不见了。

鹧鸪天·座中有眉山隐客史应之和前韵即席答之·黄菊枝头生晓寒
黄庭坚

　　黄菊枝头生晓寒。人生莫放酒杯干。风前横笛斜吹雨，醉里簪花倒著冠。

　　身健在，且加餐。舞裙歌板尽清欢。黄花白发相牵挽，付与时人冷眼看。

Partridges in the Sky
Huang Tingjian

On yellow chrysanthemums dawns the morning chill.
Do not let your wine cup go dry while you live still!
Play on your flute when slants the rain and blows the breeze!
Drunk, pin a flower on your invert hat with ease!

When you keep fit, eat better meal and drink more wine!

Enjoy your fill with dancers sweet and songstress fine!

As golden blooms become the young, white hair the old.

Why should I care for other people's glances cold?

关键词

pin: 作动词时，有"别上"意。"簪花"是中国古代人头饰的一种，故译者用 pin a flower 对译之，十分贴切。

care for: 关心。"我为何要关心别人的冷眼呢？"译者以反问句对译"付与时人冷眼看"，加强肯定语气，体现了词人挣脱世俗约束的高旷理想。

译文

黄菊枝头生出阵阵寒意。人生苦短，莫让酒杯空，请开怀畅饮。迎着斜风细雨吹笛奏乐，趁着醉意倒戴帽子，摘一朵花插在头发上。

身体尚且健康，努力多餐。在佳人舞蹈中尽情欢乐。白发老人与年少佳人挽手，任他们冷眼相看。

卜算子·兰·松竹翠萝寒

曹组

松竹翠萝寒，迟日江山暮。幽径无人独自芳，此恨凭谁诉？
似共梅花语，尚有寻芳侣。着意闻时不肯香，香在无心处。

Song of Divination

Cao Zu

You are cold among pines, bamboos and vines.

When over the land the setting sun shines.

Alone you're fragrant on a lonely lane.

To whom of your loneliness can you complain?

With the mume blossoms you may speak,

Whom lovers of flowers might seek.

But you would not exude fragrance to please;

It can't be sought for as the breeze.

关键词

vines：葡萄藤。

loneliness：孤独，对译"恨"。译者结合全词的意境，将词人的"恨"具化为志节坚芳而寂寂无闻的"孤独"，直译为"你的孤独又能向谁说"。

exude：散发出。此句是全词的警句，直译为"但你不会散发出芬芳来取悦别人"，幽香可以为人无心领略，却不可有意强求，词人高洁之怀得表。

sought for：寻求，寻找。

译文

山间的傍晚苍茫远淡，松竹和藤蔓都添了一丝寒意。幽深的小径旁，只有兰花独自散发着芳香，它心中的幽怨又可以向谁诉说呢？

也许它可以将心事说与梅花听，这山间应该还有寻访赏花之人。特意闻兰花的时候花并不香，不经意间却又闻到它的幽香。

曹 组

曹组，字彦章，颍昌（今河南许昌）人，一说阳翟（今河南禹县）人。因占对才敏，深得宋徽宗宠幸，奉诏作《艮岳百咏》诗。存词三十六首，近人赵万里编为《箕颍词》，以"侧艳"和"滑稽下俚"著称，在北宋末年传唱一时。

辑
五

半
城

烟
沙

念奴娇·赤壁怀古·大江东去
苏轼

大江东去，浪淘尽，千古风流人物。故垒西边，人道是：三国周郎赤壁。乱石穿空，惊涛拍岸，卷起千堆雪。江山如画，一时多少豪杰。

遥想公瑾当年，小乔初嫁了，雄姿英发。羽扇纶巾，谈笑间，樯橹灰飞烟灭。故国神游，多情应笑我，早生华发。人生如梦，一樽还酹江月。

Charm of a Maiden Singer
Thinking of Ancient in Red cliff
Su Shi

The endless river eastward flows;
With its huge waves are gone all those

Gallant heroes of bygone years. West of the ancient fortress appears

Red Cliff where General Zhou won his early fame

When the Three Kingdoms were in flame.

Rocks tower in the air and waves beat on the shore,

Rolling up a thousand heaps of snow.

To match the land so fair, how many heroes of yore, Had made a great show!

I fancy General Zhou at the height

Of his success, with a plume fan in hand,

In a silk hood, so brave and bright, Laughing and jesting with his bride so fair,

While enemy ships were destroyed as planned

Like castles in the air. Should their souls revisit this land,

Sentimental, his bride would laugh to say:

Younger than they, I have my hair turned grey.

Life is but like a dream. O moon, I drink to you who have seen them on the stream.

关键词

won his early fame: 声名鹊起之地，对 Red Cliff(赤壁)的补充，点出了三国时期赤壁之战的典故。

gallant heroes: 伟大的英雄，对译 "风流人物"。与后文的 heroes of yore (昔日的英雄，对译 "豪杰") 相呼应，再现了周瑜等历史上的风流人物指点江山、建功立业的威武形象。

as planned：直译为"正如计划的一样"，此处译文着意加词，点出了诸葛亮的运筹帷幄。

his bride：他的新娘，代指小乔。此处译者以人物的身份代替了人名，更为简洁，运用了归化的翻译策略，即以目标文化为导向。前文的 general Zhou（以周将军代指周瑜）亦同，也是运用归化策略，点明了人物身份，更符合英语国家的人物介绍习惯，也增添了历史韵味。

译文

大江之水滚滚东去，巨浪滔滔淘尽千古英雄。西边遗留下来的营地，人们说三国时，周郎在此驻扎，大破曹军。岸边乱石林立，惊人的巨浪拍打悬崖，雪白的浪花好像千万堆白雪。江山壮丽如画，一时间涌现出多少英雄豪杰。

回想起当年的周瑜，与小乔新婚燕尔，英姿雄健见识卓越。手摇羽扇，头绑丝巾，谈笑之间，便将敌人的战船烧得灰飞烟灭。如今我身临古战场神游往昔，可笑我有如此多的怀古柔情，却已有白发。人生如同一场梦，且用一杯好酒洒在地上以祭奠明月。

江城子·密州出猎·老夫聊发少年狂
苏轼

老夫聊发少年狂，左牵黄，右擎苍。锦帽貂裘，千骑卷平冈。为报倾城随太守，亲射虎，看孙郎。

酒酣胸胆尚开张，鬓微霜，又何妨？持节云中，何日遣冯唐？会挽雕弓如满月，西北望，射天狼。

Riverside Town

Hunting at Mizhou

Su Shi

Rejuvenated, I my fiery zeal display;

On left hand leash, a yellow hound,

On right hand wrist, a falcon grey.

A thousand silk-capped, sable-coated horsemen sweep

Across the rising ground, And hillocks steep.

Townspeople pour out of the city gate

To watch the tiger-hunting magistrate.

Heart gladdened with strong wine, who cares

About a few new-frosted hairs?

When will the court imperial send

An envoy to recall the exile? Then I'll bend

My bow like a full moon, and aiming northwest, I

Will shoot down the fierce Wolf from the sky.

关键词

tiger-hunting：猎虎。对译"亲射虎，看孙郎"，此处为浅化或一般化的译法。词人以少年英主孙权自比，更显"狂"劲和豪兴，译者未直译孙郎之名，以"射虎"这一共同举动代之。

gladden：使……喜悦。heart gladdened with strong wine，对译"酒酣胸胆尚开张"，直译为"酒浓心畅"。

new-frosted：直译为"新染霜的"头发，全句以 a few 和 new 一起对译"鬓微霜"之"微"，又以 frosted 译白发，比之 white 更准确。

译文

且让我抒发一下少年壮志，左手牵着黄犬，右手托着苍鹰，头戴华帽身穿皮草，带着大部队浩浩荡荡踏平山冈，尘土飞扬。替我转告全城百姓，随我出城打猎，看我亲射猛虎。

我酣畅饮酒，心有远志，忠肝义胆。两鬓微微发白又有何妨？皇帝什么时候派遣人拿着符节去边地云中，就像汉文帝派遣冯唐一样？我定会拉满弓弦，将箭瞄准西北部队。

满江红 · 怒发冲冠
岳飞

怒发冲冠，凭阑处、潇潇雨歇。抬望眼、仰天长啸，壮怀激烈。三十功名尘与土，八千里路云和月。莫等闲、白了少年头，空悲切。

靖康耻，犹未雪。臣子恨，何时灭。驾长车，踏破贺兰山缺。壮志饥餐胡虏肉，笑谈渴饮匈奴血。待从头、收拾旧山河，朝天阙。

The River All Red
Yue Fei

Wrath sets on end my hair; I lean on railings where
I see the drizzling rain has ceased.
Raising my eyes, Towards the skies, I heave long sighs,
My wrath not yet appeased.

To dust is gone the fame achieved in thirty years;

Like cloud-veiled moon the thousand-mile Plain disappears.

Should youthful heads in vain turn grey, We would regret for aye.

Lost our capitals, What a burning shame!

How can we generals, Quench our vengeful flame!

Driving our chariots of war, we'd go, To break through our relentless foe.

Valiantly we'd cut off each head; Laughing, we'd drink the blood they shed.

When we've reconquered our lost land,

In triumph would return our army grand.

关键词

appeased：安抚。对译"壮怀激烈"，此处为意译，直译为"我的愤怒还未平息"，译者以否定句式对译，凑了韵，也加强了语气。

burning shame：奇耻巨辱。靖康之耻，指徽钦两帝被掳，犹不得还，对臣子而言，自是奇耻大辱，故译者以感叹句式对译，将词人的愤怒与沉痛刻画得入木三分。

relentless：残酷无情的。此句对译"踏破贺兰山缺"，贺兰山在西北，为攻打匈奴之处，译者在此以浅化手法直译为"大破我们那残酷无情的敌人"，更明白易懂。

译文

我气愤得头发竖起来将帽子高高顶起，凭栏远眺，一场骤急的雨刚刚停歇。抬头眺望天空，不由得长叹一声，报国之情涌上心头。三十多年来虽然建立了一些功名，但如同尘土般微不足道，四处奔波转战的八千里路，只有同行的云与月记得。不要虚度年华消磨人生，等到黑发变白发，只有悔恨悲伤。

靖康之变的耻辱，至今还未洗雪，作为社稷臣子的愤恨，什么时候才可以泯灭。我要驾驭战车向敌方进军，将贺兰山踏为平地。胸怀壮志的将士饿了就以敌人的肉为食，在谈笑间渴了就喝敌人的血。等到我重新收复这残破的山河，再进京朝拜官家，报告胜利的消息。

岳　飞

　　岳飞，字鹏举，相州汤阴（今河南汤阴县）人。南宋时抗金名将，民族英雄，位列南宋"中兴四将"之首。且文才卓越，文学造诣也相当高，其代表词作《满江红·怒发冲冠》，笔力雄健，是千古传颂、脍炙人口的名篇佳构。

小重山 · 昨夜寒蛩不住鸣
岳飞

昨夜寒蛩不住鸣。惊回千里梦，已三更。起来独自绕阶行。人悄悄，帘外月胧明。

白首为功名。旧山松竹老，阻归程。欲将心事付瑶琴。知音少，弦断有谁听？

Manifold Little Hills
Yue Fei

The autumn crickets chirped incessantly last night,
Breaking my dream homebound; It was already midnight.
I got up and alone in the yard walked around;
On window screen the moon shone bright;
There was no human sound.

My hair turns grey. For the glorious day.

In native hills bamboos and pines grow old.

O when can I see my household?

I would confide to my lute what I have in view,

But connoisseurs are few.

Who would be listening, Though I break my lute string?

关键词

homebound：归家。该句对译"惊回千里梦"，直译为"打破了我归家（收复失地）的梦"。译者将 homebound 作为后置定语，内容贴切，且和下文的 around 押尾韵。

household：家庭，家人。该句对译"阻归程"，此处为意译，直译为"我何时才能见到我的家人呢"。以疑问语气反衬了归乡之难，也和 old 押韵。

译文

昨天夜里蟋蟀不停地鸣叫，惊扰了我回千里外的家乡的美梦，醒来时已经三更天了。没有困意的我起身绕着院子踱步，四周静悄悄的，只有帘子外一轮皎月朦朦胧胧。

从青丝到华发都是为了建功立业名留青史，故里的松竹都已苍老，我却被琐事阻碍了返乡的归程。想把满腹心事都通过弹瑶琴诉说出来，可是知音难觅，琴弦弹断又有何人听得出来呢？

破阵子·为陈同甫赋壮词以寄之·醉里挑灯看剑

辛弃疾

　　醉里挑灯看剑，梦回吹角连营。八百里分麾下炙，五十弦翻塞外声，沙场秋点兵。

　　马作的卢飞快，弓如霹雳弦惊。了却君王天下事，赢得生前身后名。可怜白发生！

Dance of the Cavalry

Xin Qiji

Though drunk, we lit the lamp to see the glaive;

Sober, we heard the horns from tent to tent.

Under the flags, beef grilled, Was eaten by our warriors brave

And martial airs were played by fifty instruments:

It was an autumn manoeuvre in the field.

On gallant steed, Running full speed,
We'd shoot with twanging bows
Recovering the lost land for the sovereign,
It is everlasting fame that we would win.
But alas! White hair grows!

关键词

sober：未喝醉的、清醒的，与上文的 drunk（酒醉）相对，对译"梦回（此处为梦醒，回到梦里之意）"。

recovering the lost land：收复失地，此处为意译，直接点明"君王的天下事"。

but alas：but（但是），一个转折，前文铺垫已久的豪情被生生截住；alas（唉），一声悲叹，壮志难酬、英雄迟暮的悲愤、可惜之情顿生。

译文

两盏热酒下肚，拨亮灯火，拔出宝剑细细观摩，梦中好像回到了战场上，听到了军营里的号角声。让部下分食牛肉，让军歌响彻塞外。这是秋天里阅兵的日子。

战马像的卢马那样跑得飞快，弓箭声像惊天的雷声。一心想替君主完成恢复中原之事，取得世代流传的美名。可惜人已白头。

永遇乐·京口北固亭怀古·千古江山
辛弃疾

千古江山，英雄无觅孙仲谋处。舞榭歌台，风流总被雨打风吹去。斜阳草树，寻常巷陌，人道寄奴曾住。想当年，金戈铁马，气吞万里如虎。

元嘉草草，封狼居胥，赢得仓皇北顾。四十三年，望中犹记，烽火扬州路。可堪回首，佛狸祠下，一片神鸦社鼓。凭谁问：廉颇老矣，尚能饭否？

Joy of Eternal Union
Think of Ancient in the Northern Tower
Xin Qiji

The land is boundless as of yore,
But nowhere can be found

A hero like the king defending southern shore.

The singing hall, the dancing ground,

All gallant deeds now sent away

By driving wind and blinding rain!

The slanting sun sheds its departing ray

O'er tree-shaded and grassy lane

Where lived the Cowherd King retaking the lost land.

In bygone years,

Leading armed cavaliers,

With golden spear in hand,

Tigerlike, he had slain

The foe on the thousand-mile Central Plain.

His son launched in haste a northern campaign;

Defeated at Mount Wolf, he shed his tears in vain.

I still remember three and forty years ago

The thriving town destroyed in flames by the foe.

How can I bear

To see the chief aggressor's shrine

Worshipped' mid crows and drumbeats as divine?

Who would still care

If an old general

Is strong enough to take back the lost capital?

关键词

driving wind, blinding rain: 强劲的风、茫茫大雨, 疾风骤雨, 对译"雨打风吹", driving, blinding 两个形容词的附加, 更精准地传达原词的意境。

launch in haste: 匆忙地发动进攻, 对译"仓皇北顾"。该句主语 his son 直接点出了人物关系, "元嘉"是刘裕之子刘义隆的年号, 此处为"元嘉"的意译, 利于理解。

take back: 拿回, 夺回, 以 take back the lost capital(收复河山), 对译老将军"尚能饭否", 也未译廉颇, 而说 an old general, 表意准确且更通俗易懂。

译文

千年江山, 再也找不到像孙权那样的英雄。舞榭歌台仍在, 英雄传说却被历史消磨殆尽。斜阳照着草树横生的普通小巷, 人们都说那是刘裕曾经住过的地方。回想当年, 他领着千军铁马收复失地, 气势如虎。

元嘉二十七年, 宋文帝盲目北伐, 贪功冒进, 大败而归。我来到这里已经四十三年了, 还记得当年战事不断, 抗争连年不绝。可现在, 当地老百姓只把佛狸祠当作一位神祇来奉祀供奉, 而不知道它过去曾是一个皇帝的行宫。更没有人会问一句：廉颇老了, 饭量还好吗？

青玉案·元夕·东风夜放花千树
辛弃疾

东风夜放花千树，更吹落，星如雨。宝马雕车香满路。凤箫声动，玉壶光转，一夜鱼龙舞。

蛾儿雪柳黄金缕，笑语盈盈暗香去。众里寻他千百度，蓦然回首，那人却在，灯火阑珊处。

Green Jade Cup
The Lantern Festival
Xin Qiji

One night's east wind adorns a thousand trees with flowers
And blows down stars in showers.
Fine steeds and carved cabs spread fragrance en route;
Music vibrates from the flute; The moon sheds its full light,

While fish and dragon lanterns dance all night.

In gold-thread dress, with moth or willow ornaments,

Giggling, she melts into the throng with trails of scents.

But in the crowd once and again

I look for her in vain. When all at once I turn my head,

I find her there where lantern light is dimly shed.

关键词

the moon: 月亮，对译"玉壶"，在原词中，玉壶即指月亮，此处未直译，而取其本来的意象。

giggling: 咯咯地笑，对译"笑语盈盈"，"盈盈"摹状，"咯咯"摹声。

melt into: 融入，对译"暗香去"，直译为"融入衣香飘散的人群中"。

once and again: 一次又一次地，再三，对译"千百度"，千回百回，把这个概数前移，置于动作 look for 之前，且另排一行，以示强调。

译文

东风趁着夜色卷落千树繁花，又将漫天的烟花吹如雨下。豪华的马车跑过，留下满路的芳香。悠扬的音乐随风远传，光影流转，鱼形和龙形的灯笼像鱼龙闹海一样舞动一夜。

街上的美人们带着华丽的饰物，笑语盈盈地穿过人群，身后暗香浮动。我在人群中焦急地寻找他的身影。猛然回头，才发现那人就站在灯火零落的地方。

扬州慢·淮左名都
姜夔

淳熙丙申至日，予过维扬。夜雪初霁，荠麦弥望。入其城，则四顾萧条，寒水自碧，暮色渐起，戍角悲吟。予怀怆然，感慨今昔，因自度此曲。千岩老人以为有"黍离"之悲也。

淮左名都，竹西佳处，解鞍少驻初程。过春风十里。尽荠麦青青。自胡马窥江去后，废池乔木，犹厌言兵。渐黄昏，清角吹寒，都在空城。

杜郎俊赏，算而今、重到须惊。纵豆蔻词工，青楼梦好，难赋深情。二十四桥仍在，波心荡、冷月无声。念桥边红药，年年知为谁生。

Slow Song of Yangzhou

Jiang Kui

In the famous town east of River Huai
And scenic spot of Bamboo West,

Breaking my journey,I alight for a short rest.

The three-mile splendid road in breeze have I passed by;

It's now overgrown with wild green wheat and weeds.

Since Northern shore was overrun by Jurchen steeds,

Even the tall trees beside the pond have been war-torn.

As dusk is drawing near,

Cold blows the born;

The empty town looks drear.

The place Du Mu the poet prized,

If he should come again today,

Would render him surprise.

His verse on the cardamon spray

And on sweet dreams in mansions green

Could not express

My deep distress.

The Twenty-four Bridges can still be seen,

But the cold moon floating among

The waves would no more sing a song.

For whom should the peonies near

The bridge grow red from year to year?

关键词

scenic spot: 风景区，此句对译"竹西佳处"。竹西，亭名，在扬州东蜀岗上禅智寺前，风光优美。译者直译"竹西"为

Bamboo West，但加了 scenic spot 补充说明。

overgrown：蔓生的，杂草丛生的。"荞麦青青"易让人想起"彼黍离离"的诗句，并从"青青"所特有的一种凄艳色彩，加强了故国之情。故译者基于原词的感情基调，用了 overgrown 一词，给人无限萧条之感。

distress：忧虑、悲伤。此句对译"难赋深情"，译者将此"情"具体化，译作 distress，此情无其他，实在是哀深恨彻。

no more：不再。此句对译"波心荡、冷月无声"，为意译，直译为"可是冷月之间浮动，海浪不再唱歌了"。

译文

扬州是著名的都会，这里有游览胜地竹西亭。我在这里稍作停留。曾经热闹繁华的扬州，如今长满了青青的荞麦。自从金兵入侵江南，洗劫扬州后，这里只剩废旧的池台和枯槁的老树，让人不愿谈起战争。临近黄昏，清冷的号角声在这空城的上空回响。

杜牧俊逸清赏，就算他今日重到此地，也会感到震惊。即使"豆蔻"词语精工，青楼美梦的诗意很好，也难抒写此刻深沉悲怆的感情。二十四桥依旧还在，桥下水波荡漾，明月高挂无言。想那桥边红色的芍药花，年年为谁而开？

姜 夔

　　姜夔，字尧章，号白石道人，饶州鄱阳（今江西上饶市鄱阳县）人。精通音律，能自度曲，其词格律严密，涉猎甚广，多寄意抒怀、感时伤世之作，清虚骚雅，刚劲疏宕，自成一家，是继苏轼之后又一难得的艺术全才。著有《白石道人诗集》《白石道人歌曲》等。

南乡子·诸将说封侯
黄庭坚

重阳日，宜州城楼宴，即席作。

诸将说封侯，短笛长歌独倚楼。万事尽随风雨去，休休，戏马台南金络头。

催酒莫迟留，酒味今秋似去秋。花向老人头上笑，羞羞，白发簪花不解愁。

Song of a Southern Country
Written on Mountain-climbing Day
Huang Tingjian

Generals talks of nobility or long;

I lean on balustrade, listening to flute song.

Everything will be gone with wind and rain,

In vain, in vain! The golden bridle of the steed can't long remain.

Drink wine without delay!

It tastes as good now as last Mountain-Climbing Day.

Flowers would smile on an old man's head,

Blush and go red. To rid of grief white hair with flowers will be wed.

关键词

remain：留下，遗留。can't long remain，意为"无法长留"，此处暗含南朝宋武帝刘裕欢宴重阳这一典故，该句译文进行了浅化，只说当年的戏马台上如今也只剩下了马笼头，道出了词人的悲凉凄苦之情。

blush and go red：blush 本为"脸红"意，译者又叠加一脸红"go red"，合起来对译"羞羞"，并且凑到了 red 和 head、wed 押韵，体现了音律之美。

译文

将军们议论封侯之事，我却独倚高楼，短笛长歌。就让世间万事随风而去，刘裕在重阳登临戏马台，与群臣宴会的盛景已一去不复返了。

劝你饮下这杯美酒，今年的酒跟去年一样醇香。花儿在老人头上羞笑，满头白发簪花也不消解忧愁。

诉衷情 · 当年万里觅封侯
陆游

当年万里觅封侯，匹马戍梁州。关河梦断何处？尘暗旧貂裘。
胡未灭，鬓先秋，泪空流。此生谁料，心在天山，身老沧洲。

Telling the Innermost Feeling
Lu You

Alone I went a thousand miles long, long ago
To serve in the army at the frontier.
Now to the fortress town in dream I could not go,
Outworn my sable coat of cavalier.

The foe not beaten back,
My hair no longer black,

My tears have flowed in vain.

Who could have thought that in this life I would remain

With a mountain-high aim

But an old mortal frame!

关键词

frontier: 边境，对译"梁州"。梁州治所在南郑，在陆游著作中，称其参加四川宣抚使幕府所在地，常杂用以上地名。故译者在此将其浅化，以边境译之。全句均为意译，直译为"在边境的军队中服役"。

a mountain-high aim: 此处"天山"并非实指，而是一种夸张的用法，指目标之高远，故译者以"山一样高的目标"译之。

译文

回想当年奔赴万里疆场建功立业，单枪匹马戍守梁州边境。如今边疆要塞的从军生活只能出现在梦里。貂裘落满灰尘，再无光泽。

入侵者还未打败，鬓边先生白发，只能空流泪。谁能料到我此生，心在边疆，人却困在沧洲。

点绛唇 · 金谷年年
林逋

金谷年年，乱生春色谁为主？余花落处，满地和烟雨。
又是离歌，一阕长亭暮。王孙去，萋萋无数，南北东西路。

Rouged Lips
Lin Bu

In the garden, from year to year,
When spring runs riot, green grass will appear.
The ground covered with fallen blooms,
In mist and rain grass looms.

Again we sing the farewell song,
At dusk in the Pavilion Long.

Gone is my friend.

The grass still grows north, south, east, west without end.

关键词

riot: 放纵，恣意。runs riot 对译"乱生"。原词写春色用"乱生"二字，可见荒芜之状，译者以 riot 点出杂树横空、蔓草遍地之状，自然引出下文"园子荒凉无主"之语。

Pavilion: 亭，阁。Pavilion long，长亭。译者将修饰词后置，使得 long 与 song 押韵。且古代为亲人送行，常长亭设宴饯别，吟咏留赠，故译者将"长亭"等化译出。

译文

金谷园年年杂草乱生，这春色谁来做主？枝头残留的花瓣，在细细的烟雨中飘落满地。

又响起离别的歌曲，送行的人在这里话别。离人走远，萋萋芳草铺满了前行之路。

水调歌头·定王台·雄跨洞庭野
袁去华

雄跨洞庭野，楚望古湘州。何王台殿，危基百尺自西刘。尚想霓旌千骑，依约入云歌吹，屈指几经秋。叹息繁华地，兴废两悠悠。

登临处，乔木老，大江流。书生报国无地，空白九分头。一夜寒生关塞，万里云埋陵阙，耿耿恨难休。徒倚霜风里，落日伴人愁。

Prelude to Water Melody

Prince Ting's Terrace

Yuan Quhua

Towering over the lakeside

In ancient southern state far and wide,

Whose palace hall is it? And by which prince?

Its base still stands a hundred feet high since.

I fancy a thousand steeds with rainbow flags proud

And songs and music waft into the cloud.

How many autumns have passed so fast!

I sigh over the magnificent capital.

Over its rise and fall!

Where I climb high,

Old is the tree,

The great river flows by.

What can I do to make our motherland free?

Nine-tenths of my hair have grown white,

The cold invades the frontier overnight.

The palaces proud are buried for miles in cloud.

How can my wrath be done?

In vain I'm lost in wind and frost.

My grief is only shared by the setting sun.

关键词

waft：飘荡，吹拂。此句对译"依约入云歌吹"，直译为"还有急管高歌吹拂入云"。

wrath：愤怒，盛怒，对译"恨"——词人报国无门，故土难收的悲愤，译者用词准确，且以问句对译陈述句，加强了"恨难休"的语气。

is only shared by：此句对译"落日伴人愁"，直译为"只有夕阳分享我的恨愁"，译者加了 only 一词，写尽词人的落寞和孤独，全词以天涯孤影的悲凉画面结束。

译文

定王台位于湘楚大地，雄踞洞庭湖之滨。这座楼台是何人所建？那高百尺的台基可以追溯到西汉年间，修建者是西汉定王刘发。想当年这里一定是宝马雕车旌旗招展，丝竹弦乐声声直抵云霄。几度岁月过去，繁华盛景不再，兴盛衰落无常。

登台远望，只见高大的树木凋零，长江滚滚东流，看到此情此景，不禁感叹自己空有满腔热血却报国无门，徒生白发。寒风一夜间侵入边疆，皇家陵阙都湮没在万里层云中，每想到此都耿耿于怀悲愤难休。然而我做不了什么，只能徒步行走在凛冽寒风中，唯有夕阳与我相伴，更添几分忧愁。

袁去华

袁去华，字宣卿，江西奉新（一作豫章）人，约宋高宗绍兴末前后在世。善为歌词，尝为张孝祥所称。著有《适斋类稿》《袁宣卿词》《文献通考》，今存词九十余首。

水龙吟 · 落叶 · 晓霜初著青林

王沂孙

晓霜初著青林，望中故国凄凉早。萧萧渐积，纷纷犹坠，门荒径悄。渭水风生，洞庭波起，几番秋杪。想重涯半没，千峰尽出，山中路、无人到。

前度题红杳杳。溯宫沟、暗流空绕。啼螀未歇，飞鸿欲过，此时怀抱。乱影翻窗，碎声敲砌，愁人多少。望吾庐甚处，只应今夜，满庭谁扫？

Water Dragon Chant

To Fallen Leaves

Wang Yisun

The green forest is lost in morning frost;

I think my homeland should look sad and drear.

Shower by shower you pile up high,

Leaves on leaves fall and sigh,

On the lane or before the door.

On the stream the breeze blows;

In the lake the waves roar,

Deeper and deeper autumn grows.

You cover half the hills high and low,

Bare peaks appear,

On mountain path few come and go.

No more verse on red leaf flows

From palace dike down

To wind around an empty town.

Cicadas trill without cease,

High up fly the wild geese,

They seem to know how my heart sighs.

How much it grieves

To see the shadow of falling leaves

And hear the sound when they scratch the ground.

I stretch my eyes

To see leaves cover my cot before the day.

Who will sweep them away?

关键词

leaves on leaves: 叶子叠着叶子，对译"纷纷"，摹叶落状，与上文的 shower by shower 对仗工整。

　　roar：呼啸。此句对译"洞庭波起"，译者以 the lake 浅化译洞庭湖，便于理解，以摹声的 waves roar（波浪呼啸），对译摹状的湖波汹涌。

　　verse：题诗。此句对译"前度题红杳杳"，原指的是唐宣宗时，中书舍人卢渥红叶题诗的典故，以此暗示故宫的冷落。译者浅化译之，"再也没有人在宫堤下流出的红叶上题诗了"，将朝代更迭的感慨表达得淋漓尽致。

　　stretch：使变大。此句为意译，直译为"我睁大了双眼，看头天落下的满庭落叶，如今又有谁来扫"，stretch my eyes 画龙点睛，悲愁与惆怅，哀怨与孤独之情尽出。

译文

　　早上的寒霜刚刚攀上青色的树叶，眼里的故国也早是一片荒凉。地上的落叶堆积，树上的叶子欲坠，大门破败，小路静悄悄的。渭水起风，洞庭荡波，几年暮秋了。想到重重叠叠的山被落叶覆盖，千峰已裸露出来。山中的路，却无人可以到。

　　从前题红之事已不再见，顺着宫沟而上，流水空绕。蝉鸣还未停歇，鸿雁欲飞，此时心怀感叹。杂乱的树叶落于窗前，树叶被踩碎的声音敲打宫墙，多少愁苦之人。遥望我家在哪里？只是今夜，满院的落叶谁来扫？

王沂孙

　　王沂孙，字圣与，号碧山，会稽（今浙江绍兴）人。工词，含蓄深婉处类周邦彦，清峭处又颇似姜夔，与周密、张炎、蒋捷并称"宋末四大家"。有词集《碧山乐府》，存词六十余首。

青玉案 · 被檄出郊题陈氏山居 · 西风乱叶溪桥树

张榘

西风乱叶溪桥树。秋在黄花羞涩处。满袖尘埃推不去。马蹄浓露，鸡声淡月，寂历荒村路。

身名多被儒冠误。十载重来漫如许。且尽清樽公莫舞。六朝旧事，一江流水，万感天涯暮。

Green Jade Cup
Written on a Hill House
Zhang Ju

Leaves fallen from the creekside trees, Run riot in the breeze;
I see autumn in yellow chrysanthemums shy.
How can I clean my dusty sleeves?

Horse hoofs seem lost, In heavy frost,

The village on lonely pathway grieves,

Cocks crow at the waning moon in the sky.

Rank and fame are not won, By the hard-working one.

Ten years later I come again, slow I remain.

Do not dance but drink your cup dry.

The splendor of six dynasties is gone in vain

With the running water of the stream.

I feel on earth all like a dream.

关键词

shy：害羞，羞涩。词人的"羞涩"两字极妙，既写出此黄花经过一夜浓霜摧打，尚未抬起头来，有些羞答答的神态，又表现出词人羞愤苦涩的心情。傲霜独开的菊花在一夜的摧打之后也不免"羞涩"，花犹如此，人何以堪！故译者等化译之，保留了原词的"炼字"之美。

like a dream：像一个梦，对译"万感天涯暮"之"暮"。"暮"在此不仅指物理时间上的黄昏，也是词人感叹国家命运已近黄昏，故译者将本句意译为"万事如梦"。

译文

西风吹乱溪桥边的树叶。菊花仿佛害羞地低着头，尽显秋日萧瑟。满身尘埃，怎么都拂之不去。晓行的马匹踏着浓重的露水，远处晨鸡在月亮逐渐消失时就开始打鸣，我一人身处这荒村，满怀孤寂。

　　身世与名利都被这官帽拖累，十年后重游此地竟有如此多的感慨。暂且饮尽杯中酒，且莫高兴。六朝更迭只换来一江流水，让人无限感慨时光易逝，人生无常。

张 镃

张镃，字方叔，号芸窗，南徐（今江苏镇江）人，约宋宁宗嘉定初前后在世。著有《芸窗词稿》一卷，《四库总目》传于世。

月上瓜洲·南徐多景楼作·江头又见新秋
张辑

江头又见新秋，几多愁？塞草连天何处是神州？
英雄恨，古今泪，水东流。惟有渔竿明月上瓜洲。

The Moon over Melon Islet
The Multi-scene Tower
Zhang Ji

How much grief to see the autumn wind blows
By the riverside again!
Frontier grass skyward grows.
Where's the lost Central Plain?

Our heroes' tear on tear,

Though shed from year to year,

With the eastward-going river flows.

Only the moonshine

With my fishing line

On Melon Islet goes.

关键词

Melon Islet: Melon，瓜，Islet，小岛，对译"瓜洲"，此处为直译。本词原调名为《乌夜啼》，词人取末句意改为《月上瓜洲》。故译者为尊重词人更改的曲调名，做了直译。

from year to year: 该句对译"古今泪"，此处为意译，译者用 tear on tear, from year to year 两个对仗押韵的短句回应了原词的对仗，直译为"我们的英雄年复一年地泪流满面"。

译文

江边新增的秋色，带来几多新愁？秋草连天，故国尚在何处？

英雄怀恨，古今多少英雄泪，都随江水东流去。眼前只有瓜洲明月，江上鱼竿。

张 辑

　　张辑，字宗瑞，鄱阳（今江西鄱阳县）人。得诗法于姜夔。黄升《中兴以来绝妙词选》卷九云："有词二卷，名《东泽绮语债》，朱湛卢为序，称其得诗法于姜尧章，世所传《欸乃集》，皆以为采石月下谪仙复作，不知其又能词也。其词皆以篇末之语而立新名云。"

水调歌头·把酒对斜日
杨炎正

把酒对斜日，无语问西风。胭脂何事，都做颜色染芙蓉。放眼暮江千顷，中有离愁万斛，无处落征鸿。天在阑干角，人倚醉醒中。

千万里，江南北，浙西东。吾生如寄，尚想三径菊花丛。谁是中州豪杰，借我五湖舟楫，去作钓鱼翁。故国且回首，此意莫匆匆。

Prelude to Water Melody
Yang Yanzheng

Wine cup in hand,I face the slanting sun;
Silent,I ask what the western wind has done.
Why should the rouge redden lotus in dye?

I stretch my eye, To see the evening river far and wide,

Brimming with parting grief, Beyond belief,

Where no message-bearing wild geese can alight.

Beyond the balustrade extends the sky.

I lean on it, halfdrunk and halfawake.

For miles and more, Over the north and south

Of the river mouth, And east and west of the river shore,

I roam like a parasite.

Thinking of the chrysanthemums along the pathways,

Who is so generous in those days

To lend me a boat to float on the lake, Or fish by riverside?

Turning my head to gaze on the lost land,

How could I, doing nothing, here stand!

关键词

brimming: 满溢的。斛，古代容量单位，十斗为一斛，后改为五斗一斛。"万斛"，比喻愁多。故译者以"满溢的"来修饰愁。

alight: 飞落。

message-bearing wild geese: 对译"征鸿"——远飞的大雁，译者将"鸿雁"这个具体的意象等化译之，与全词愁绪满怀的沉郁基调一致。

parasite: 寄生，依赖他人过活者。

gaze on: 凝视。直译为"我回头凝视着失落的故土"，以"凝视"译"回望"，准确译出了词人对故国的深情。

译文

我举起酒杯敬夕阳，默然无语问东风。为什么胭脂将荷花染得这般红。眺望这暮色中的千顷江水，里面有万斛的离别愁绪，远飞的鸿雁也没有地方可以落脚。天空在阑干的一角，我却在半醉半醒间。

辗转千万里，到过大江南北，也走遍浙西浙东。我一生漂泊，仍在想三径旁的菊花丛。谁是中原的豪杰，借我舟楫泛游五湖，做一个闲散的钓翁。回望故国，这种想法太匆匆。

杨炎正

杨炎正，字济翁，庐陵（今江西吉安）人，杨万里族弟，与辛弃疾交谊甚厚。工词，有《西樵语业》一卷存世，《四库总目提要》称其词"纵横排之气，虽不足敌弃疾，而屏绝纤秾，自抒清俊，要非俗艳所可拟"。

辑六

思归

念远

踏莎行 · 郴州旅舍 · 雾失楼台
秦观

雾失楼台，月迷津渡，桃源望断无寻处。可堪孤馆闭春寒，杜鹃声里斜阳暮。

驿寄梅花，鱼传尺素，砌成此恨无重数。郴江幸自绕郴山，为谁流下潇湘去？

Treading on Grass
Qin Guan

Bowers are lost in mist;

Ferry dimmed in moonlight,

Peach Blossom Land ideal is beyond the sight.

Shut up in lonely inn, can I bear the cold spring?

I hear at lengthening sunset homebound cuckoos sing.

Mume blossoms sent by friends

And letters brought by post,

Nostalgic thoughts uncounted assail me oft in host.

The lonely river flows around the lonely hill.

Why should it southward flow, leaving me sad and ill?

关键词

dimmed: 变模糊，对译"迷"，辨认不清。月色朦胧，让往日繁华的渡口也隐匿不见了，为后文深深的离恨起势。

shut up: 闭嘴，明明是孤身一人独居客栈而无人对谈，却以凌厉的"闭嘴"一词来译，更显被迫之情，离恨之深。

southward flow: 向南流，对译"流下潇湘去"，词人才贬郴州，又贬横州，看到郴江之水的流动，不禁想到自身。译诗"意美"的"深层义"可见。

译文

暮霭沉沉，楼台消失在浓雾中，月色朦胧，渡口也隐匿不见。望断天涯，也找不到心中的桃花源。无奈只能独自在客栈忍受春寒，杜鹃在夕阳里声声鸣啼。

远方亲友遥寄温暖的问候，却平添了我深深的离恨。连郴江都耐不住寂寞，不然为什么要流到潇湘去呢？

千秋岁 · 水边沙外

秦观

水边沙外。城郭春寒退。花影乱，莺声碎。飘零疏酒盏，离别宽衣带。人不见，碧云暮合空相对。

忆昔西池会。鹓鹭同飞盖。携手处，今谁在？日边清梦断，镜里朱颜改。春去也，飞红万点愁如海。

A Thousand Autumns

Qin Guan

Beyond the sandbar by the waterside,

Out of the town the spring chill begins to subside.

The flowers' shadows running riot, The orioles' warble breaks

the quiet.

Lonely, I drink few cups of wine, My belt loosens, for friends I pine.

But where are they? In vain clouds gather up at the end of the day.

I still remember our Western Pool's rendezvous:

Together with our cabs herons and egrets flew.

Where we stood hand in hand, Who still stays in that land?

My dream can't fly to sunny place; The mirror shows my wrinkled face.

Away spring's sped; My grief looks like a sea of falling petals red.

关键词

lonely: 孤独的，寂寞的，此处为意译，以孤独说"飘零"，译者不拘泥于具体用词，而将情绪具体化，直指情绪内核。

hand in hand: 携手。与后文的"in that land"押韵，此为"音美"；且两个分句遵循了原词的对仗，此为"形美"。

wrinkled face: 长了皱纹的脸庞，对译富含中国文化背景的"朱颜改"。"长满皱纹的脸庞"比"年轻美好的面容已改变"更具象、更震撼。

译文

溪水边，沙洲外，春天的寒意从这城郊悄然退去。花影迷乱，鸟声打破了宁静。风雨飘摇的生活使我不能借酒消愁，思念之苦让我衣带渐宽。友不见，我只能和蓝天暮霭相对无言。

回想起与诸同僚相聚金明池，乘车出游。可如今，我们一同走过的地方，还有谁在？京都帝王的好梦破灭，镜中的容颜渐老。春光消逝，落花飘零，愁思无边。

蝶恋花·密州上元·灯火钱塘三五夜
苏轼

灯火钱塘三五夜。明月如霜，照见人如画。帐底吹笙香吐麝，更无一点尘随马。

寂寞山城人老也。击鼓吹箫，却入农桑社。火冷灯稀霜露下。昏昏雪意云垂野。

Butterflies in Love with Flowers

Lantern Festival at Mizhou

Su Shi

On Lantern Festival by riverside at night,

The moon frost-white

Shone on the beauties fair and bright.

Fragrance exhaled and music played under the tent,

The running horses raised no dust on the pavement.

Now I am old in lonely hillside town,

Drumbeats and flute songs up and down

Are drowned in prayers amid mulberries and lost.

The lantern fires put out, dew falls with frost.

Over the fields dark clouds hangs low: It threatens snow.

关键词

on Lantern Festival：元宵节，此处为意译，对译"灯火"。译文结合了原词的写作背景，点明了时间和灯火之来源。

It threatens snow：要下雪了，对译"昏昏雪意"。threatens 被威胁，预示着。郊外彤云四垂，阴霾欲雪。意象凄清，与上阕杭州的元宵节形成鲜明对比。

译文

杭州城里的元宵节好热闹，明月高挂，如霜的月光将行人照成一幅画。有钱人家的帐内吹笙乐入耳，焚麝香幽香入鼻。街道上气清土润，行马无尘。

寥落的密州里只剩下老人，人们击鼓吹箫，最后只会去农桑社祭莫土地神。灯火稀少冷清，寒露降下，昏沉的乌云笼罩着田野，要下雪了。

西江月 · 黄州中秋 · 世事一场大梦
苏轼

世事一场大梦，人生几度新凉？夜来风叶已鸣廊，看取眉头鬓上。

酒贱常愁客少，月明多被云妨。中秋谁与共孤光，把盏凄然北望。

The Moon over the West River
The Mid-autumn Moon in Huang zhou
Su Shi

Like dreams pass world affairs untold,

How many autumns in our life are cold!

My corridor is loud with wind-blown leaves at night.

See my brows frown and hair turn white!

Of my poor wine few guests are proud;

The bright moon is oft veiled in cloud.

Who would enjoy with me the mid-autumn moon lonely?

Winecup in hand, northward I look only.

关键词

autumns：秋天。译者参照原词的写作时间——中秋，以秋凉对译"新凉"。全句直译为"人生能有几个秋"。

frown：皱眉，蹙额。该句对译"看取眉头鬓上"，frown、turn white 均为译者加词深化，将意象具体化，且做到了句尾押韵。

译文

世间事不过只是一场梦，人生还能经历几度凉意初透的秋？夜里，风吹动树叶的声音响彻回廊。愁思停留在眉间，白发早已爬上鬓边。

美酒价贱，买的人却不多。明月虽白，却多被烟云遮蔽。中秋之夜，谁与我共赏这天上的孤月。我只能举起酒杯，惆怅地看向北方。

临江仙 · 送钱穆父 · 一别都门三改火
苏轼

一别都门三改火，天涯踏尽红尘。依然一笑作春温。无波真古井，有节是秋筠。

惆怅孤帆连夜发，送行淡月微云。樽前不用翠眉颦。人生如逆旅，我亦是行人。

Riverside Daffodils
Farewell to a Friend
Su Shi

Three years have passed since we left the capital;
We've trodden all the way from rise to fall.
Still I smile as on warm spring day.
In ancient well no waves are raised;

Upright, the autumn bamboo's praised.

Melancholy, your lonely sail departs at night;

Only a pale cloud sees you off in pale moonlight.

You need no songstress to drink your sorrow away.

Life is like a journey; I too am in my way.

关键词

from rise to fall: 起起落落。译者将状语后置，加强 all 的含义，对译"踏尽红尘"。

drink your sorrow away: 直译为"喝掉你的悲伤"，此处为意译，对译"樽前……翠眉颦"。此句译者将"翠眉"译为 songstress（女歌手、歌妓），为浅化。

译文

京城一别已是三年，你辗转天涯经历这么多，相见时依然能笑得像春天般温暖。你的内心就像古井一样毫无波澜，你的品格像秋天的竹竿一样高风亮节。

离别让人惆怅，你连夜就要乘船出发，送行时月光不明，天抹微云。我们都不用紧锁眉头。人生就像一个客栈，我只是路过的行人。

水调歌头·明月几时有
苏轼

丙辰中秋，欢饮达旦，大醉，作此篇，兼怀子由。

明月几时有？把酒问青天。不知天上宫阙，今夕是何年？我欲乘风归去，又恐琼楼玉宇，高处不胜寒。起舞弄清影，何似在人间？

转朱阁，低绮户，照无眠。不应有恨，何事长向别时圆？人有悲欢离合，月有阴晴圆缺，此事古难全。但愿人长久，千里共婵娟。

Prelude to Water Melody

Su Shi

How long will the full moon appear?

Wine cup in hand,I ask the sky.

I do not know what time of year

It would be tonight in the palace on high.

Riding the wind, there I would fly,

Yet I'm afraid the crystalline palace would be

Too high and cold for me.

I rise and dance, with my shadow I play.

On high as on earth,

would it be as gay?

The moon goes round the mansions red

Through gauze-draped windows to shed

Her light upon the sleepless bed.

Against man she should have no spite.

Why then when people part, is she oft full and bright?

Men have sorrow and joy; they part or meet again;

The moon is bright or dim and she may wax or wane.

There has been nothing perfect since the olden days.

So let us wish that man

Will live long as he can!

Though miles apart,

we'll share the beauty she displays.

关键词

gay: 轻松的，无忧无虑的。此句对译"何似在人间"，直译为"天上和人间一样，都会快乐吗"。原词中并未详说词人的内心情感，译者用了 gay 一词，不仅凑了韵，也表达了词人的情感。

gauze-draped windows：对译"绮户"。gauze 原指窗纱，drape 为悬挂之意，在极具中国特色的事物的翻译上，译者最大限度地写出了原词的实景，具象可观。

shed her light upon the sleepless bed：对译"照无眠"，译者巧妙地运用了转喻，用 sleepless bed 指代离人，给人更多思考和遐想的空间。

oft：时常，古语或诗歌用语，等于 often。此处为怅恨久别，用埋怨的口吻对月亮无可奈何地发问。

译文

这样的明月几时还能再有？我举起酒杯遥问青天。不知天宫现在是什么日子。我想乘着风上天去看看，又担心华丽的天宫太高，我经受不了寒冷。我翩翩起舞，身影随动。天宫哪里比得上人间滋味？

月儿移动，转过了朱红色的阁楼，低低地挂在雕花的窗户上，照着没有睡意的人。月儿不该对人们有什么怨恨吧，为什么总是在分离的时候圆呢？人间有悲欢离合，月亮有阴晴圆缺。人月团圆的事情千古以来难以两全。只愿两情长久，虽隔千里，也能共赏明月。

南乡子·集句·怅望送春怀
苏轼

怅望送春杯。渐老逢春能几回。花满楚城愁远别，伤怀。何况清丝急管催。

吟断望乡台。万里归心独上来。景物登临闲始见，徘徊。一寸相思一寸灰。

Song of the Southern Country

Su Shi

Wine cup in hand,I see spring off in vain.

How many times can I,grown old,see spring again?

The town in bloom,I'm grieved to be far,far away.

Can I be gay?

The pipes and strings do hasten spring not to delay.

I croon and gaze from Homesick Terrace high;

Coming for miles and miles, alone I mount and sigh.

Things can be best enjoyed in a leisurely way;

For long I stay,

And inch by inch my heart burns into ashes grey.

关键词

gaze：凝视，注视，对译"望"。译者未用"看"，而用凝视，更能凸显词人强烈的思念故土之情。

ashes：灰烬，此句对译"一寸相思一寸灰"。词人辗转反侧，心如寒灰，译者以 heart burns into ashes grey（心烧成了灰烬）对译，实景化的翻译，意境和情感都得以传达。

译文

惆怅地看着手中的送春酒，日渐年迈又能再逢几个春天。我在这繁花似锦的黄州为远离亲人而愁，伤心。连酒筵上的清丝急管都演奏起思乡之曲。

登高饮酒，思乡情切。纵使与家乡相隔万里，仍归心似箭。这些景色待我无官一身轻时才登高观赏，徘徊不前。思乡之情让我辗转反侧，心如寒灰。

苏幕遮 · 碧云天
范仲淹

碧云天，黄叶地，秋色连波，波上寒烟翠。山映斜阳天接水，芳草无情，更在斜阳外。

黯乡魂，追旅思，夜夜除非，好梦留人睡。明月楼高休独倚，酒入愁肠，化作相思泪。

Waterbag Dance
Fan Zhongyan

Clouds veil emerald sky,Leaves strewn in yellow dye.

Waves rise in autumn hue

And blend with mist cold and green in view.

Hills steeped in slanting sunlight, sky and waves seem one;

Unfeeling grass grows sweet beyond the setting sun.

A homesick heart,When far apart,

Lost in thoughts deep,

Night by night but sweet dreams can lull me into sleep.

Don't lean alone on rails when the bright moon appears!

Wine in sad bowels would turn to nostalgic tears.

关键词

dye：染料，染液。此句对译"黄叶地"，直译为"落叶被染成了黄色"。一个"dye"将"碧云天"和"黄叶地"连成了一片，构成了一个更空旷辽远的情境，别情愁绪也点染得更为浓烈。

lull：使昏昏欲睡。lull me into sleep 对译"留人睡"，译者加了 lull 这个动词，强调了只有"好梦"能让"我"入眠。

rail：栏杆。译者以栏杆代指高楼，是对 lean alone on（独倚）的一个补充，情境更为具体可感。

nostalgic：思乡的，对译"相思"，译者准确地点出了此处的相思无它，乃思乡也，此处翻译用了深化之法。

译文

蓝天白云，黄叶满地，秋色接着江波，江面青烟后是苍翠的远山。斜阳映照在山上，水面接天。芳草比人更无情，一直延绵到斜阳之外。

思念家乡让人黯然神伤，撇不开羁旅的愁思。除非夜夜好梦，才能让人安心入眠。明月当空，独坐高楼，喝下消愁的苦酒，却又化成相思泪。

范仲淹

范仲淹,字希文,苏州吴县(今江苏苏州)人。北宋杰出的文学家、政治家。他倡导的"先天下之忧而忧,后天下之乐而乐"思想和仁人志士节操,对后世影响深远,有《范文正公文集》传世。

苏幕遮·燎沉香
周邦彦

燎沉香，消溽暑。鸟雀呼晴，侵晓窥檐语。叶上初阳干宿雨，水面清圆，一一风荷举。

故乡遥，何日去？家住吴门，久作长安旅。五月渔郎相忆否？小楫轻舟，梦入芙蓉浦。

Waterbag Dance
Zhou Bangyan

I burn an incense sweet, To temper steamy heat.
Birds chirp at dawn beneath the eaves,
Announcing a fine day. The rising sun
Has dried last night's raindrops on the lotus leaves,
Which, clear and round, dot water surface. One by one

The lotus blooms stand up with ease

And swing in morning breeze.

My homeland's far away; When to return and stay?

My kinsfolk live in south by city wall.

Why should I linger long in the capital?

Will not my fishing friends remember me in May?

In a short-oared light boat, it seems,

I'm back' mid lotus blooms in dreams.

关键词

announcing：通告、宣布，对译"呼"字。该句直译为"黎明，鸟儿在檐下叽叽喳喳的，宣告着一个好天气"。旧有"鸟鸣可占晴雨"之说，译者在此浅化译之。

kinsfolk：亲属。此句对译"家住吴门"，古吴县城亦称吴门，即今之江苏苏州，此处以吴门泛指江南一带。故译者以"亲属住在南方城市"和"我长久在长安"做对比，更显离愁之深。

linger long：长久地逗留。译者以 linger（流连、逗留）一词点明词人"旅人"之身份，十分贴切。

译文

　　焚烧沉香，消除潮湿的暑气。鸟雀呼唤着晴天，拂晓时，我在屋檐下偷听它们窃窃私语。新出的阳光晒干了荷叶上昨晚下的雨，水面上的荷花清润饱满，迎着晨风舞动。

什么时候才能回到遥远的故乡？我家远在江南，却长年在长安当异客。又到五月，不知家乡的朋友是否也在想念我。梦里，我划着一叶小舟，回到了西湖。

周邦彦

周邦彦，字美成，号清真居士，钱塘（今浙江杭州）人。精通音律，曾创作不少新声词调，作品多写闺情、羁旅，也有咏物之作。格律谨严，语言曲丽精雅，长调尤善铺叙，在婉约派词人中被尊为"正宗"。有《清真居士集》，已佚，今存《片玉集》。

卜算子慢 · 江枫渐老
柳永

江枫渐老，汀蕙半凋，满目败红衰翠。楚客登临，正是暮秋天气。引疏砧、断续残阳里。对晚景、伤怀念远，新愁旧恨相继。

脉脉人千里。念两处风情，万重烟水。雨歇天高，望断翠峰十二。尽无言、谁会凭高意？纵写得、离肠万种，奈归云谁寄？

Slow Song of Divination
Liu Yong

The riverside maples grown old, Sweet orchids wither by and by.

The faded red and green spread out before the eye.

A Southerner,I climb up high; It's already late autumn cold.

The setting sun is drowned

In washerwoman's intermittent pounding sound.

With evening scenery in view,

Though far away, can I not think of you?

How can old grief not be followed by sorrow new?

Silent,a thousand miles separate you and me.

In two places our dreams, Can't fly o' er streams on streams.

When stops the rain, the sky's serene;

My eyes can't go beyond the twelve peaks green.

Wordless, who would understand my

Leaning on railings at the height?

Though I can write, Down parting grief with broken heart,

Would clouds return and bring it for my part?

关键词

by and by: 逐渐。译者以 grown old 译"渐"老，以 by and by 译"半"凋。

Southerner: 南方人，对译"楚客"。此处引用宋玉《九辩》悲秋之意，柳永曾宦游于荆襄一带的古代楚地，故这里自称为"楚客"。译者则运用浅化手法，以南方人对译楚客。

be followed by: 紧随其后的是。此句对译"新愁旧恨相继"，直译为"怎样才能让新伤不跟着旧恨而来呢？"译者以问句译陈述句，语气加强，伤感之情骤升。

for my part: 对我来说，就我而言。此句对译"奈归云谁寄"，无乘归去之云的人寄送鸿信，无可奈何之情被倾吐而出。且句尾

part 与上文的 heart 押韵。

译文

江边的枫叶逐渐衰老，水洲的芳草半已凋零，满眼都是衰败的红花绿叶。楚乡作客，登高望远，正逢晚秋。稀疏的捣衣声，断断续续地回响在夕阳里。面对这傍晚的景象，我思念家乡，新愁和旧恨，接连涌起。

思念之人远在千里。两处相思，相隔千山万水。雨后的天空辽阔，能看到最远的十二座苍山。无言相诉，谁会登高抒意？纵使写出离别的断肠愁苦，无奈谁能驾驭行云帮我把情书寄给相思之人？

诉衷情近·雨晴气爽

柳永

雨晴气爽，伫立江楼望处。澄明远水生光，重叠暮山耸翠。遥认断桥幽径，隐隐渔村，向晚孤烟起。

残阳里。脉脉朱阑静倚。黯然情绪，未饮先如醉。愁无际。暮云过了，秋光老尽，故人千里。竟日空凝睇。

Telling Innermost Feeling

Liu Yong

The air is fresh on a fine day after the rain,
I stand in a riverside tower and gaze.
Afar the water stretches clear and bright,
Green hills on hills tower in the twilight.
I find the broken bridge and quiet lane

In fisher's village veiled in haze,

At dusk I see lonely smoke rise.

Seeing the sun sink, Silent I lean on railings red,

With sorrow fed, I'm drunk before I drink.

Boundless is my grief cold,

Evening clouds pass before my eyes.

Autumn turns old.

My friends stay miles away;

In vain I gaze all the long day.

关键词

gaze：凝视，第一处对译"望"，与下文的 haze 押韵；第二处对译"凝睇"，为等化译之。原词中"凝睇"与开头的江楼"伫望"首尾圆合，浑然一体，译者则在这两处都用了 gaze 一词，切合了原词之意。

haze：烟雾。veiled in haze，掩藏在烟雾之中，译者将状语后置，对译"隐隐"渔村。

all the long day：全天候的，一整天，对译"竟日"。英语中一般以 all day long 来译整天，此处译者故意将 long 前置，使得 day 与上文的 away 押韵。

译文

雨过天晴，天气清爽，伫立在江边高楼远望。远处的水面波光清澈，重叠的苍山高耸青翠。眺望中辨认出西湖断桥，幽深小路，隐隐的渔村，及傍晚时分升起的炊烟。

　　夕阳里，我含情倚靠楼阑，心情沮丧，酒没下肚人先醉。这愁无边无际。黄昏的云飘过，秋日的光景殆尽，古人遥隔千里。我只能整天凝睇无语。

八声甘州·对潇潇暮雨洒江天
柳永

对潇潇暮雨洒江天，一番洗清秋。渐霜风凄紧，关河冷落，残照当楼。是处红衰翠减，苒苒物华休。唯有长江水，无语东流。

不忍登高临远，望故乡渺邈，归思难收。叹年来踪迹，何事苦淹留？想佳人妆楼颙望，误几回、天际识归舟。争知我，倚栏杆处，正恁凝愁！

Eight Beats of Ganzhou Song
Liu Yong

Shower by shower
The evening rain besprinkles the sky
Over the river,
Washing cool the autumn air far and nigh.

Gradually frost falls and blows the wind so chill

That few people pass by the hill or rill.

In fading sunlight is drowned my bower.

Everywhere the red and the green wither away;

There's no more splendor of a sunny day.

Only the waves of River Long

Silently eastward flow along.

I cannot bear

To climb high and look far, for to gaze where

My native land is lost in mist so thick

Would make my lonely heart homesick.

I sigh over my rovings year by year.

Why should I hopelessly linger here?

From her bower my lady fair

Must gaze with longing eye.

How oft has she mistaken home bound sails

On the horizon form mine?

How could she know that I,

Leaning upon the rails,

With sorrow frozen on my face, for her I pine!

关键词

besprinkles：洒，散布。besprinkles the sky over the river，对译"洒江天"，暮雨洒遍了江天。

the hill or rill：那山川或溪流，此句对译"关河冷落"，直译为"无论是山川还是溪流，都鲜有人经过"。因前文用 few people（几乎没有人）这一否定词，故后文用了 or 连接山川溪流来对译"关河"。

splendor：壮丽，壮观。此句对译"苒苒物华休"，直译为"不再有壮丽的晴日"。"苒苒"意同"渐"，一切美好的事物渐渐地衰残，其中寓有无穷的感慨愁恨。

pine：难过，悲伤。此句对译"正恁凝愁"，正如此忧愁凝结不解。for her I pine，译者引出对象，为了她我如此难过，让忧愁凝结在了脸上。

译文

傍晚时分，潇潇暮雨在辽阔的江天飘洒，看这一番被雨洗过的残秋。秋风渐渐凄凉紧迫，山河凋敝，落日余晖映照着江楼。到处都花叶凋零，美好的景物已成过去。只有长江水，沉默东流。

不忍心登高望远，看到家乡渺茫遥远，想家的思绪难以平复。感叹近年奔波流浪，究竟是什么让我在这里停留。佳人一定在高楼眺望，多少次错把远处驶来的船只当作心上人的归舟。谁知我正在倚栏远眺，因思乡愁苦不已。

卜算子·送鲍浩然之浙东·水是眼波横
王观

水是眼波横，山是眉峰聚。欲问行人去那边？眉眼盈盈处。

才始送春归，又送君归去。若到江南赶上春，千万和春住。

Song of Divination

Par with Bao Haoran to the East of Zhe Jiang

Wang Guan

The rippling stream's a beaming eye;

The arched brows are mountains high.

May I ask where you're bound?

There beam the eyes with arched brows around.

Spring's just made her adieu,

And now I'll part with you.

If you overtake Spring on southern shore,

Oh, stay with her once more!

关键词

beaming eye：笑眼，对译"眼波横"，"水是眼波横"即"水像美人流动的眼波"。译者以笑眼译脉脉传情的眼波，形象传神。

adieu：再见，告别。原词是"送春归"，春为被动，译文则用了一个被动语态 made her adieu，准确译出"送"字的言下之意——春归人也归，词人此行是愉快的。

译文

水像美人流动的眼波，山似美人蹙起的眉峰。想问行人要去哪里？只道山水交汇的地方。

刚刚把春送走，又要送君归去。如果你到了江南赶上春天，一定要把春天留住。

王 观

　　王观，字通叟，如皋（今江苏南通如皋）人。相传曾奉诏作《清平乐》，描写宫廷生活，因高太后对王安石变法甚为不满，认为王观是王安石门生，遂以其词亵渎了宋神宗为由将其罢职，此后便自号"逐客"，以布衣终老。

浣溪沙 · 春日即事 · 远远游蜂不记家

刘辰翁

远远游蜂不记家。数行新柳自啼鸦。寻思旧事即天涯。
睡起有情和画卷，燕归无语傍人斜。晚风吹落小瓶花。

Silk-washing Stream

A Spring Day

Liu Chenweng

Far away the bees roam without knowing their home;
On a few new shoots of willow trees the crows cry.
I think of the days gone by as far as the end of the sky.

Awake from sleep,I roll up my dream with my scroll.

The silent swallows come back in slanting sunrays;

The evening wind blows down flowers in a vase.

关键词

roll up：卷起。此句对译"睡起有情和画卷"，"有情"指的是上文的"寻思旧事"，译者将其译为"我用卷轴卷起了我的梦"，十分灵动。

slanting sunrays：斜阳。此句为意译，直译为"沉默的燕子在斜阳中回来了"，原词的"傍人斜（依傍着人飞）"即指日落时燕子归巢之景，故译者将其浅化译之。

译文

在春光里漫游的蜜蜂越飞越远，不知归家。几株刚发嫩芽的新柳上有几只乌鸦在啼叫，此情此景，我不由得想起了当年漂泊天涯的旧事。

午睡醒后我将画轴卷了起来，燕子在余晖中归来，贴着人无声飞行。瓶中，一朵小花的花瓣在微凉的晚风中飘落。

刘辰翁

刘辰翁，字会孟，别号须溪，庐陵（今江西吉安）人，南宋末年爱国词人。文风取法苏辛而又自成一体，豪放沉郁而不求藻饰，真挚动人。作词数量仅次于辛弃疾、苏轼。遗著有《须溪先生全集》，《宋史·艺文志》著录为一百卷，已佚。

孤雁儿 · 藤床纸帐朝眠起
李清照

世人作梅词，下笔便俗。予试作一篇，乃知前言不妄耳。

藤床纸帐朝眠起，说不尽、无佳思。沉香断续玉炉寒，伴我情怀如水。笛声三弄，梅心惊破，多少春情意。

小风疏雨萧萧地，又催下、千行泪。吹箫人去玉楼空，肠断与谁同倚？一枝折得，人间天上，没个人堪寄。

A Lonely Swan
Mume Blossoms
Li Qingzhao

Woke up at dawn on cane-seat couch with silken screen.

How can I tell my endless sorrow keen?

With incense burnt, the censer cold

Keeps company with my stagnant heart as of old.

The flute thrice played

Breaks the mume's vernal heart which vernal thoughts invade.

A grizzling wind and drizzling rain,

Call forth streams of tears again.

The flutist gone, deserted is the bower of jade.

Who'd lean with me, broken-hearted, on the balustrade?

A twig of mume blossoms broken off, to whom can I

Send it, on earth or on high?

关键词

flutist：对译原作"吹箫人"一词。"吹箫人"原指擅长吹箫的萧史。李清照引用萧史弄玉的传说，以萧史转指赵明诚。译诗则采取"移植源语转喻"的方法，用 flutist（吹箫人）这个凸显度高的属性作为转喻的喻体，再结合上下文"wind""broken-hearted"等词加以渲染，把原作对丈夫的刻骨哀思表达得淋漓尽致。

on earth or on high：在地上还是在天上？对译"人间天上"。译者用"or"一词连贯天上人间，并转换了句式，以问句译陈述句，对应了"没个人堪寄"的肯定语气，对原词的意境描述准确。

译文

早上，从薄帐里的藤床上醒来，却有一种说不尽的伤感。沉香燃尽，香炉也凉了，我的心绪如清水一样无味。《梅花三弄》的笛曲惊醒了梅花，惹来春意。

门外细雨潇潇下个不停，让人不禁又泪下千行。吹箫的人离去，只剩空楼。我的愁绪又能跟谁分享？折下一枝梅花，找遍了天上人间，却没人可让我寄赠。

四园竹·浮云护月

周邦彦

浮云护月，未放满朱扉。鼠摇暗壁，萤度破窗，偷入书帏。秋意浓，闲伫立，庭柯影里。好风襟袖先知。

夜何其。江南路绕重山，心知谩与前期。奈向灯前堕泪，肠断萧娘，旧日书辞，犹在纸。雁信绝，清宵梦又稀。

Bamboos in West Garden

Zhou Bangyan

Floating clouds protect the moon bright,
They will not let the red door be steeped in her light.
Rats under the dark wall are seen,
Through the torn window fireflies pass,
And flit in stealth by window screen.

Autumn is deep, alas! I stand on the grass

In the shade of the evergreen trees,

My sleeves feel the soft breeze.

How old is night?

A long way winds across mountains to southern shore.

How could you keep the date of yore?

How can I not shed tears by candlelight

To think with broken heart of you

And read your oldened billet-doux?

No more wild geese will bring your letter to me.

Can dreams on lonely night be free?

关键词

be steeped in: 被浸透，充满。本句直译为"浮云是不会让月亮的光辉洒满朱扉的"，译者以被动句式译出了原词"浮云护月"的拟人化意味。

flit in stealth: 秘密地掠过，对译"偷入"。译者将萤在不知不觉中进入书帏的情景再现，原词寂寞、萧索的意境尽出。

billet-doux: 情书，对译"书辞"。译者以情书译之，实为深化，结合上下文语境将这"旧日书辞"具体化，表达词人秋夜怀人之情。

译文

浮云遮住了月光，未能照满红门。老鼠在壁角肆意活动，萤火虫破窗，偷偷进入书帷。浓浓的秋色，我独自站在院中的树下。夜风穿过我的衣襟和袖口，让我感到寒意。

　　到了几更天？伊人远在江南，心里已知早先的约定已枉然。让我在灯前落泪，思念断肠，旧日书信还躺在那里。而今书信断绝，连梦中也不再出现她的身影。

唐多令·芦叶满汀洲
刘过

安远楼小集，侑觞歌板之姬黄其姓者，乞词于龙洲道人，为赋此《唐多令》。同柳阜之、刘去非、石民瞻、周嘉仲、陈孟参、孟容。时八月五日也。

芦叶满汀洲，寒沙带浅流。二十年重过南楼。柳下系船犹未稳，能几日，又中秋。

黄鹤断矶头，故人今在否？旧江山浑是新愁。欲买桂花同载酒，终不似，少年游。

Song of More Sugar
Liu Guo

Reeds overspread the small island; A shallow stream girds the cold sand.

After twenty years I pass by the Southern Tower again.

How many days have passed since I tied my boat

Beneath the willow tree! But Mid-Autumn Day nears.

On broken rocks of Yellow Crane, Do my old friends still remain?

The old land is drowned in sorrow new.

Even if I can buy laurel wine for you

And get afloat, Could our youth renew?

关键词

gird: 束、带、裹紧。此句对译"寒沙带浅流"，译者调整了语序，直译为"浅流围着寒沙流过"，意境表达得更为具体。

drowned: 淹没、浸没，对译"旧江山浑是新愁"之"浑（全是）"，直译为"新愁淹没了旧土"。

renew: 重新开始。Could our youth renew？译者以问句对译陈述句，强调"终不似"，少年豪气已不在，直译为"我们的青春能重新开始吗"。

译文

芦苇铺满了沙洲，浅浅的江水在寒沙上流过。二十年后重来南楼。柳树下的小船还未停稳，我就匆忙下船。过不了几日，又到中秋。

矶头的残垣有黄鹤停留，故人如今在哪？满目的旧景，让我平添新愁。想买上桂花美酒一起上船畅饮逍遥游，却终没有少年时的意气风发。

渔家傲·和程公辟赠别·巴子城头青草暮

张先

巴子城头青草暮，巴山重叠相逢处。燕子占巢花脱树。杯且举，瞿塘水阔舟难渡。

天外吴门清霅路。君家正在吴门住。赠我柳枝情几许。春满缕，为君将入江南去。

Pride of the Fishermen
Farewell to Cheng Gongbi
Zhang Xian

By western city wall at dusk the grass grows green,
The western hills on hills where we met form a screen.
The swallows in the nest, flowers fall from the tree.
We drink wine cup in hand,

It's hard to sail between the cliffs for our homeland

Your home at citygate and mine by riverside,
They are not separated by a river wide.
How deep your love to break a willow twig for me
It's filled with spring,
A sprig to your home on the southern shore I'll bring.

关键词

western city wall：对译"巴子城头"，巴子即今四川之巴县，渝州附近。在翻译地理名词时，若只译音则无法传达该城地理位置的特别，故译者将其浅化，以 western city 代指。下文的巴山译为 western hills，瞿塘译为 the cliffs for our homeland 亦同。

sprig：小枝，意思同上文的 twig，译者用了两个不同的单词，避免重复，代指的均是盎然的春意。此句意译为满眼绿色的柳枝飘舞，送你到江南。

译文

渝州城头长满了绿草，天色向晚，我们在重峦叠嶂的巴山相逢。你仿佛即将筑巢的燕子，而我还像一片离开树枝的花瓣在风中飘零。举杯换盏间，我们感叹着瞿塘江水面宽阔，很难渡过。

远在天外的苏州，连着通往吴兴的路，而你家正好在苏州。你折柳送我表达情深义重。这满目的春意，好像是为了送你回江南而显得盎然。

踏莎行·祖席离歌
晏殊

祖席离歌，长亭别宴。香尘已隔犹回面。居人匹马映林嘶，行人去棹依波转。

画阁魂消，高楼目断。斜阳只送平波远。无穷无尽是离愁，天涯地角寻思遍。

Treading on Grass
Yan Shu

The farewell song is sung for you;

We drink our cups and bid adieu.

I look back though fragrant dust keeps you out of view.

My horse going home neighs along the forest wide,

Your sailing boat will go farther with rising tide.

My heart broken in painted bower,

My eyes worn out in lofty tower,

The sun sheds departing rays on the parting one.

Boundless and endless will my sorrow ever run;

On earth or in the sky it will never be done.

关键词

bid adieu: 告别。原词的前两句用了互文的手法，"祖席""离歌""别宴"说的实为一事，故译者特地选用了 bid adieu 来译告别，两句均用了七个单词，对仗整齐，且 adieu 与 you 押韵。

rising tide: 涨潮，本句对译"行人去棹依波转"，直译为"你的行船随着潮水渐行渐远"，未译"去棹"，而"去棹"之意全出。

boundless and endless: 对译"无穷无尽"。boundless，无限的，无边无际的；endless，无穷尽的，译者用一个 and 将两词连接，从时空上加强了这"离愁"的深远。

译文

在长亭设宴饯别，酒席上离歌已唱过，带着香气的尘土遮挡了离人回首的视线。送行人的马在林中嘶叫，远行人的船已随江波渐远。

画阁里我魂牵梦萦，高楼上我望断天涯。夕阳下江波荡到天边。离愁无穷无尽，我只想寻遍天涯海角。

浪淘沙 · 把酒祝东风
欧阳修

把酒祝东风，且共从容。垂杨紫陌洛城东。总是当时携手处，游遍芳丛。

聚散苦匆匆，此恨无穷。今年花胜去年红。可惜明年花更好，知与谁同？

Sand-sifting Waves
Ouyang Xiu

Wine cup in hand, I drink to the eastern breeze:
Let us enjoy with ease!On the violet pathways
Green with willows east of the capital,
We used to stroll hand in hand in bygone days,
Rambling past flower shrubs one and all.

In haste to meet and part, Would ever break the heart.

Flowers this year

Redder than last appear.

Next year more beautiful they'll be.

But who will enjoy them with me?

关键词

the capital：首都，对译"洛城（即洛阳）"。译者不直译洛阳，而浅化译作首都，更便于读者理解。

stroll：漫步。此句对译"总是当时携手处"，直译为"那是我们常常携手漫步的老地方"。译者加了 stroll 一词，不仅使句末的 days 与上文的 pathways 押韵，还与下文的 rambling（同为"漫步"义）做了区分，避免重复，十分精巧。

译文

端起酒杯向东风祈祷，请你再多留些时日，不要着急离去。杨柳枝垂满了洛阳城东郊外的小道，就是我们去年携手共同游览过的地方，那里的花丛姹紫嫣红。

人生聚散匆匆，让人苦恼，离别遗憾更是在心中无穷无尽。今年的花比去年更鲜艳，明年的花一定会开得更灿烂，可惜那时，还有谁与我同赏呢？

一剪梅·舟过吴江·一片春愁待酒浇

蒋捷

一片春愁待酒浇。江上舟摇，楼上帘招。秋娘渡与泰娘桥，风又飘飘，雨又萧萧。

何日归家洗客袍？银字笙调，心字香烧。流光容易把人抛，红了樱桃，绿了芭蕉。

A Twig of Mume Blossoms

My Boat Passing by Southern River

Jiang Jie

Can boundless grief be drowned in spring wine?

My boat tossed by waves high,Streamers of wineshop fly.

The Farewell Ferry and the Beauty's Bridge would pine:

Wind blows from hour to hour;

Rain falls shower by shower.

When may I go home to wash my old robe outworn,

To play on silver lute, And burn the incense mute?

Oh, time and tide will not wait for a man forlorn:

With cherry red spring dies,

When green banana sighs.

关键词

shower by shower：对译"萧萧"。"萧萧"形容雨声，暮声；译者以 shower（阵雨、一阵阵的）译之，摹状，读来视觉和听觉上的美感兼具，且有一种节奏美。

spring dies：春天消逝。原词化抽象的时光为可感的意象，以樱桃和芭蕉的颜色变化渲染出时光的飞逝，译者则加词 spring dies 和 sighs（叹息）将意象落实到情感，抒发了年华易逝、人生易老的感慨。

译文

春日里的忧愁只待用美酒消除。江上轻舟慢摇，酒楼上酒旗揽客。船只经过吴江渡和泰娘桥。春风拂过，落雨潇潇。

什么时候才能回到家乡？在家调弄有银字的笙，焚烧心字形的香。时光流转，让人追不上。樱桃才熟，芭蕉就绿了。

蒋 捷

　　蒋捷，字胜欲，号竹山，阳羡（今江苏宜兴）人。与周密、王沂孙、张炎并称"宋末四大家"，其词多抒发故国之思、山河之恸，尤以造语奇巧之作，在宋代词坛上独树一帜。南宋覆灭后，深怀亡国之痛，隐居不仕，人称"竹山先生""樱桃进士"。有《竹山词》存世。

图书在版编目（CIP）数据

　　许渊冲：枕上宋词 / 许渊冲译. -- 北京：中国致公出版社，2022

　　ISBN 978-7-5145-1821-4

　　Ⅰ．①许… Ⅱ．①许… Ⅲ．①宋词—选集 Ⅳ．①I222.844

　　中国版本图书馆CIP数据核字(2021)第033678号

许渊冲：枕上宋词 / 许渊冲 译
XU YUANCHONG:ZHENSHANG SONGCI

出　　版	中国致公出版社	
	（北京市朝阳区八里庄西里100号住邦2000大厦1号楼西区21层）	
出　　品	湖北知音动漫有限公司	
	（武汉市东湖路179号）	
发　　行	中国致公出版社　（010-66121708）	
作品企划	知音动漫图书·文艺坊	
策　　划	李　潇	
责任编辑	方　莹　胡梦怡	
责任校对	吕冬钰	
装帧设计	李艺菲	
责任印制	程　磊	
印　　刷	长沙鸿发印务实业有限公司	
版　　次	2022年11月第1版	
印　　次	2022年11月第1次印刷	
开　　本	960 mm×640 mm　1/16	
印　　张	21.25	
字　　数	257千字	
书　　号	ISBN 978-7-5145-1821-4	
定　　价	59.80元